MISSWIRED

TARA MAKHMALI

COPYRIGHT

First Printing, 2017

ISBN 978-0-9991790-0-0 (ebook)
ISBN 978-0-9991790-1-7 (print)

CommonSmarts Media, LLC
P.O. Box 5089
Hoboken, NJ 07030

MISSWIRED

"Who am I, standing in the midst of all this thought-traffic?"
—*Rumi*

PART ONE

PART ONE

CHAPTER ONE

THE RELEVANCE OF TRUTH

To inhale a moment of quiet in New York City is to catch a whisper from a tornado. I have caught the whisper. I have been kissed by a sun shower. Manhattan splatters. The scores of pedestrians, tourists, and panhandlers have parted, allowing me to fly through the city streets with ease, with solace, with bliss. But just as I cross away from Gramercy Park, a woman with copper hair appears out of nowhere and elbows me in the chest as though by intention, as though to mock this lottery-ticket win of arm's space that the Empire State Gods have temporarily endowed upon us.

"Watch it," I say. "That hurt."

"It was an accident," she replies. "Love always hurts."

"What? Who said anything about love?"

"True," she responds. "It could've been the tequila. Or the oysters. Or any number of last night's aphrodisiacs."

Now my heart is racing. "Who are you? How do I know you? Have you been following me?" As I inspect her dilated pupils, it quickly becomes apparent that she too is in awe of this emancipating day, and wants nothing more than to rejoice.

That's the story I tell myself.

"The city is ours!" she exults, singing and chortling. "Do you want to join me? Let's dance!"

"Join you?" I stand back and laugh with a healthy combination of trepidation and curiosity, until the idiot from the high-rise balcony above us flicks his lit cigarette, and it briefly scalds my jaw before landing in front of my Burberry-clad feet.

When I glance back up, the woman is halfway down the street. Her shoes have come off and so has her top. A redhead. A cigarette. *Now what*, I wonder, *an outline of a body?*

Then it hits me like a baseball bat.

Sophie.

And without warning, so it begins. My brain spirals into a recurring dream, and weaves into a neglected memory, where I am spinning, dancing arm-in-arm with a fairy. Cupid. He breaks free of my arm, and snickers as he pulls back his bow and releases his arrow in an effortless bullseye right into my heart. But when his syringe of euphoria is supposed to pierce through my chest and I am supposed to levitate, I instead crack, and the arrow—*his* arrow—drops and keeps dropping through me in a never-ending descent. I am now the arrow, sinking indefinitely, no end in sight, suspended in time, enveloped in her presence. Sophie and I sit together at the town pool. The day is scorching hot, the kind of day that grows warmer when the gusts come. Sweat is dripping off her rib cage, off her curves. She glistens. Her hair bounces over her collarbone, over her freckles. She slinks casually into her plastic pool chair. Her mouth is pursed around a clove cigarette, and smoke rings are sailing from her lips. Everyone is swirling between us—my father, the lifeguards, a cheerful repertoire of families. We splash and laugh in unfettered glee, unattuned and unsuspecting of the scream behind Sophie's blackened eye, which, between fashionable sunglasses and meticulously dabbed makeup, paints a Monet-like image. Up close, my stomach churns.

Before I lose my lunch, the sun pokes holes through the clouds, through my memories, through my dream. A ray catches my eyes off guard. I return to the present. My eyes flutter. I have stumbled into a puddle.

I refrain from cursing and instead breathe deeply.

I am supposed to be happy, for I am in love, aren't I?

I can neither confirm nor deny this.

The street comes alive with Broadway actors. Cupid's arrow has landed, but it is unclear whether it has fallen too close to the tree or too far from it. All I can think is: Was the hope of love what killed Sophie? Am I, too, fooling myself? A puddle is never *just a puddle* in New York City, and so too I realize that a memory is never just a memory; a dream, never just a dream.

***

On a humid day, between the sticky air and the aftertaste of peach schnapps, the nostalgia of teenage angst spontaneously emerged in a man who assumed he was immune to such trivial afflictions. He was a talented and educated married man with two daughters. I'm Lanna Zar, and I *was* one of them. The other is Mary, my older sister, and as you'll soon come to see, she is my dearest friend and closest confidant.

My father, Jack Zar, was a scientist, and a man of modest means and humble intentions. He spent most of his waking life scribbling down observations about unusual mold formations into his pocket-sized Moleskine notebooks—a gift from my perceptive mother, the only woman prior to Sophie to ever bat a feathered eyelash in his peculiar direction.

The four of us (Mother, Mary, Father, and I) lived in a small lakeside community in rural New Jersey with a public college that admitted anyone who thought to apply, and where Father both worked and learned. According to the townspeople, highbrows didn't much appreciate the school; it was unranked and didn't open doors for you. The teachers were students, and the students were regarded as teachers, and if you showed up late or unannounced to class, you started the semester off at a disadvantage, since the questions you posed, and more importantly, the way you impacted your surroundings, were how your peers would evaluate you. This thoughtful approach didn't appeal to the wealthy snobs that dominated the upper rungs of academia.

This was an ideal situation for my pragmatic father. He was naturally even-keeled and courteous, and believed that a solid education reconciled what one experienced as truthful with what actually was true, since, as he puts it now, "We are all bred with some inherent bias." And, as emotions and observations didn't always line up in his head the way he wanted them to, he trusted that the system would keep him and them, the students, honest and equal. Particularly since, at the end of each semester, the student with the highest marks in class was awarded the high distinction of *professor*, and as quickly as the changing seasons—the smell of pine, the sight of rusted leaves, the spectacular blooms of cherry blossoms—so, too, did the title reset back to *student*.

In hindsight, this academic upbringing could have been as much of a curse for Father as it had been a blessing, and once you've had an opportunity to reflect upon the remainder of our story, you might agree. It was probably a blessing and curse for me too, though the verdict is still out on that one.

The campus's Olympic-sized swimming pool sat unobstructed on the outskirts of town, high above the lake where the views of the Appalachian mountains were unhindered, where the white-spotted deer settled behind the shrubs of the entrance gate, and the hawks circled through the cotton-candy clouds in search of Wobbles, the lifeguard's meaty and flatulent bulldog.

Wobbles was the sort of dog everyone ogled. He had an enormous head, soft floppy ears, a massive chest, lopsided hips, and little legs that made him saunter at a constant forty-five-degree angle. He often got stuck upside down on his back like a turtle when he tried to dodge the vultures, and whoever was standing nearest to him was tasked with the courageous act of pushing him right-side up as he excreted a steady stream of gas in their general direction.

As long as you didn't stumble too close to the property's stark cliff edge—no one ever did—the pool was the town's favorite spot for summering, and in spite of the occasional poof of *Wobbles Eau de Toilette*, the air was fresh. Even if you already owned a lakefront chalet or the highly coveted in-ground pool, the way the purplish-gray mountains reached into the setting sun always gave you a feeling of inner peace.

In a town without a church, this was the easiest way to connect with whichever God or non-God you saw fit.

Our family didn't own a chalet or an in-ground pool. We lived farther into the countryside, just beyond the lake, where one day a helicopter pilot flying overhead spotted an out-of-place fig tree weaving its arms into a forest that was usually dense with pines. The pilot happened to tell my father about it, and my father knew that figs always grew near water, and there Father found an old underground cavern that was rich with microbial mold-life. That's where he chose to build our cottage, and that's where we lived.

As a teenager, I sometimes kayaked through the cavern at night. I loved what my father had loved so much about it— the glow-in-the-dark specimens that lit up the top of the water and could only be seen by the naked eye when the clouds in the night sky flirted with the yellow Moon. I always dreamed that my love life would be like that cavern— intimate, safe, mysterious, and yet, on fire. But for many years, it was far from it, the details of which I'll share some, though not all of, for what good transpires from giving stage to slimy individuals unworthy of standing in your limelight?

But enough of this digression. At five years of age, I was learning to swim. I was a beautiful catastrophe, and a bit of a late learner compared to Mary, who learned everything speedily. My wild curly-fry hair, copper-toned skin, vivacious popsicle-stained smile, muscular legs, and burgeoning curiosity made me a healthy, but more accurately, a messy, vision. It also meant I was a threat, mostly to myself, to the detriment of my parents, whose gentler introverted tendencies had not prepared them for such an outspoken-creative-athletic tornado.

The other critical impetus for my learning to swim was that Mary and I had been straying over to the water near our neighbor's chalet—usually as punishment toward our overworked mother for ignoring us as she cursed, vacuumed, mopped, and scrubbed the madness we had embedded into the walls and floors. Bouncing from rock to rock with the remnants of our pita lunches, and an assortment of twigs and pebbles that we had collected along the way, I ambitiously dangled my limber limbs over fallen shrubbery and threw leftovers to the family of geese paddling in the water.

Inevitably, I slipped in. Mother came running and screaming in the sort of hyper-panic that only a mother can, but by the time she reached us, Mary had already fished me out and was laughing hard at one of her own jokes, which later got her grounded. Pulling me out of the water, she snorted and giggled. "I bet Daddy," snort, short, snicker, snicker, "would find it fun," hee hee hee, ha ha ha, "to study the mold formation from *dead bodies*, don't you think, Mama?

DEAD BODIES," hee hee hee. "Lanna can be his first." She finished with a grin.

Mary was quickly chastised, and the next thing I knew, Father was responsible for teaching me to swim, "unless, of course," Mother had told him, "you'd like to take care of the housekeeping for the rest of us." Everyone knew he hated cleaning, and no one could blame him. We were reckless little children.

At the pool that day, I was bright-eyed, and my whimsical ruffled swimsuit made me look like a delicious strawberry—the kind of strawberry that my lanky soon-to-be-made and soon-to-be-estranged friend Sam Azurite (I'll tell you more about him later) would remember long into his elderly years. Whereas I would come to remember this summer as the summer I learned who I always was and who I was destined to be, Sam would remember it as the summer that turned him into the person he never wanted to be. It would remind him of the confusion that laced his adolescence and much of his adult life. It would remind him that the beginning of his journey through the void started with too many unanswered cries.

To say that I remember the details of that day perfectly would be a lie. And I have never been much of a liar. But, then again, what is the relevance of truth to a child who has lost his or her giver? Let's go back to that day, you and I. I'll tell you what I think I remember.

CHAPTER TWO

KICK

"I'm not ready! I'm not ready, Daddy! It's cold!" I slung my legs around Father's torso, wrapped them tightly to his waist, and hung my arms around his neck.

He struggled. "Lanna, you need to learn."

"No."

"Let go," he said firmly.

"No, I don't want to." I tightened my grip.

"Ladybug, you can't go feeding the duckies whenever you want. Don't you remember what happened last time? They all came after you at once. You could have drowned."

"Daddy, I was talking to them. They weren't going to hurt me. I told you—Mary pushed me."

"Lanna." He splashed me with water. "Don't say Mary pushed you. You know full well that she saved you. You were bouncing on the log and you bumped into her. Your mother watched the whole thing from the window. You did your little toad jump, bumped into Mary, and the whole flock got scared. And that's how you ended up with that beak mark in your calf and that goose egg on your head." He lifted my leg out of the water to look at the mark. "You're lucky, you know, that Mary is an excellent swimmer. What if she hadn't been there to rescue from the brook?"

"I don't remember seeing a goose egg. What did it look like? I would've remembered."

"Ha! You're funny, Ladybug. It's an expression. It means *a bump*, a bump on your head."

A tall boy, brown from the sun, with blue eyes and large hands, caught wind of our conversation and began smirking.

My father continued. "You know what, Ladybug; I bet you are going to be a better swimmer than Mary. She's going to be impressed with your swimming skills. Wouldn't you like that?"

I smiled at the boy. He turned away shyly and flipped open a workbook of some sort.

"Hey, look! What's that? Is that a swan? I think I see a swan. He's huge," Father exclaimed.

I spun. "Where? I don't see anything. Where is he? I want to see him."

Father quickly unlatched himself from my legs and swooshed aside.

"No! I'm not re—!" I splashed backward into the water, my body immediately shocking to the freezing cold. Before I sunk, he glided me to the edge, and I grabbed hold of the ledge.

A kickboard plopped beside me. The lifeguard walked past and winked. "That wasn't so bad, was it? You can do it, kid. Listen to your dad."

I scowled. "I don't like this."

"You'll like it. Even Wobbles likes it." Wobbles waddled over to the edge, wagged his stumpy tail, and began lapping water straight from the pool. Drool went everywhere.

"Eww, stop it, Wobbles," I said, watching him slobber, growl, and pass wind as he turned away. "Yuck." I held my breath.

Father laughed. "Good. Now that you're holding your breath, grab the board, Lanna! Do it now! Fast, like a Band-Aid."

I scurried to grab the board with one hand and then the other.

"The colder the water, the higher it needs to come up over your shoulders," he told me. "Don't worry, your body will adjust to the temperature."

I continued holding my breath.

"You're on the board. Good job! Now, kick! Exhale, Lanna. You're not underwater. Kick! Kick! Kick! Hold the kickboard to your belly and kick! Bring it closer to your belly! Head up! Kick! You're doing it. Kick! Kick!"

Bobbing up and down, gulping in water and gasping for air, I kicked tenaciously.

"C'mon, Lanna! You're doing it! Head up! If you can just get to the middle of the board, you'll be in a better position."

I lifted upward and bounced forward. I smacked the corner of the board and it darted from my hands, away from my body and into the center of the lane. "I can't reach!" I cried, stretching to it as it drifted further from my grasp.

I flailed, I kicked, I snorted, and suddenly the water felt heavy, my body felt heavy, and I couldn't stop myself from sinking into the sunlit water. And as though I were moving in slow motion and lifting out of my own body, I heard voices above me.

* * *

"Mom, your eye. It's hurt. There's a bruise there—right above your cheekbone. I can see it."

"What bruise? Oh, this old thing? It's nothing new. Don't worry about it."

"Mom! Pay attention! The girl over there—that little strawberry—she's drowning! *"Kick, little strawberry, kick! Can you hear me? Kick!"*

* * *

Adrenaline rushed through my veins. I closed my eyes and spread my wings. Within a heartbeat, Father's steady hands had wrapped themselves around my waist. He was lifting me up and pulling me out. I gasped. Air returned to my lungs. I kicked until all I could feel between my wiggling toes was air and the slippery cocoa butter on Father's smooth body.

"You look like you've seen a ghost," he said, kissing me on the cheek.

I felt like I had. "It hurts, Daddy," I whimpered. "I'm done. Done! Do you hear me? I won't do this anymore. I can't."

"Shh," he crooned gently. "You can. It's time to stop kicking."

I gradually stopped.

He squeezed me tightly. "Look at me, Ladybug."

I turned away dismissively, then looked.

"Don't panic," he said. "Panicking only makes it worse. I'm not going to let you drown; I promise. I would never put you in a situation from which you would not recover." He scanned my face. "You understand?"

I was still angry and scared. "You're a mean man!" I snapped at him. "And a bad teacher!"

"A bad student," he corrected. "How about, you be the teacher today. Can we try again?"

A breeze blew in off the lake. The sun warmed my back. The blue-eyed boy waved hello. "Keep kicking, Strawberry," he said sympathetically.

I blushed.

"Do you like that boy?" Father asked, smiling.

"Daddy. No. Yuck." My attention returned to the boy. He was again talking to his mother.

***

"Mom, what happened?" I could hear him say. He ran his fingers through her electric auburn hair, and then lowered her sunglasses to skim a finger over her eye. "Please tell me."

"Nothing happened, Sam. Don't you worry those pretty little blue eyes of yours—I made a mistake is all. I had a little fall. It's nothing." She swatted his hands off her face and slid her glasses back up her nose. Then she leaned in to kiss him on the forehead, but he skirted the kiss and instead wandered toward the corner of the pool, where he sat down and splashed his feet in the water.

***

After a deep breath, I braved up. "I'm ready," I told Father. "I'm going to try again."

"I don't blame you," he said. "I'd want to make a good impression in front of those attractive people too!"

"Daddy, stop it." I punched him in the shoulder and reddened.

CHAPTER THREE

FLOAT

Nine-year-old Sam Azurite would constantly ask his mother, "Mom, how come life doesn't have clear-cut rules like math? Why do I do everything wrong?" and whenever his mother heard him utter these nagging questions, she turned away from him in a gust of gloom, as though she too had been plagued by them.

But his father, standing tall at the bathroom mirror, grinning, and straightening his power tie before heading off to work at the bank, where he approved and rejected mortgage loans all day long, was always cheerier and much more matter of fact. "We're men, Son. We make rules; we don't abide by them," he would say.

Of course, this also confused young Sam, since he was fascinated with numbers, and in his notebook he plotted, he graphed, and he calculated. Sam carried his mathematical musings, protractor, and ruler with him wherever he went, in a small brown satchel that his mother had purchased from a local gift boutique and embroidered with his initials, and his father would scold him: "Get with the program, Sam. You can't carry a purse around. Do you want to be known as a loser or as a winner?"

If men get to make the rules, Sam wondered, *then why can't I carry my purse around?*

Thankfully, his mother found a way to sneak his satchel into her beach tote, next to her perfumes and skinny cigarettes, so that Sam had something fun to do while she sunbathed, which drove Sam's father mad, since he had strictly *prohibited* the two of them from enjoying the U-pool, claiming that Sam's mother's body was "for his" (his father's) "eyes only," and arguing, "Are you" (Sam's mother) "so pathetic that you need to flaunt your tits to all those men? Don't you have any dignity?"

Still, Sam and his mother always snuck away in the summertime when the sun was too hot to bear. Most days, sitting by the pool, Sam was content with doing nothing but linear algebra, though occasionally he encouraged a little strawberry by the name of Lanna as she learned to use a kickboard. She was a cute and silly strawberry, smart for her age, he thought, but he was sure his father would disapprove, since his father seemed to condemn everything Sam did, though it was not quite clear to him why. Sam knew it had something to do with the fact that he didn't enjoy sports like the other boys, and that he was *more like his mother*; and he was told, "You're like a girl. That's why the other children pick on you," but he didn't see himself as girly, so this was confusing. Of course, he and his mother weren't supposed to be at the pool in the first place; thus, making friends with this little strawberry and telling his father about it was a no-no, at best.

Oh, how he wished social interactions were easier to decode. He wished that all he had to do was select the right formula, plug in a couple of numbers, and, ta-da, the rest would be a cinch. Watching Lanna swim through the water, parting the lanes with her insistent forward thrusts and contagious laughter until all the other swimmers in the lane moved to other lanes and she had conquered an entire lane for herself, it was hard not to get swept away by the sweet unruliness of it.

"Kick, little strawberry, kick!" he would encourage, though sometimes his voice would crack in the middle of the "Kick" and the pretty, blonde teenage lifeguard with the gemstone nose piercing and butterfly tattoo on her back would look down upon him, and he would turn pink with embarrassment.

Strangely, by the time Lanna had finally gotten the hang of kick-boarding in the big pool without much supervision, and he had stopped paying attention, she had also grown more and more determined to get his attention. Whenever he found himself deep in mathematical modeling, it appeared she was running near or past him covered in something sticky, and then asking him questions about whether he saw her last jump; or what he thought about Wobbles; or whether he could show her his books; and why he always carried a protractor around—what did it do? *And have you tried putting a paintbrush at the end of your protractor instead of a pencil?*—which was an absurd thing to think of doing with a protractor!

And today, like many other days, she was galloping at him with her board in hand, with bug juice dripping from her lips and down onto her chin, spinning so fiercely that he swore he could see her already-curly hairs spring into another full spiral around themselves; and, hence, he shrunk backward toward the concrete and winced as she barreled her entire body at full force against him.

"Hey! Watch where you're going!" he said angrily. "Why're you always running at me?"

She was beaming. "Can I show you something?"

"What? What is it this time?"

"Why are you so afraid of the water? Didn't your daddy teach you to swim?"

He said nothing.

"What's wrong? You don't like me anymore?" she asked. "I thought you were my friend."

"No, you're a girl. I can't be friends with a girl; I already told you," he grumbled, and watched her expression fade to melancholy.

"Why not?" she demanded.

There were lots of reasons why not, but instead he paused, not knowing the right words to say. After nothing came to him, he said, "I'm not sure. Maybe it's not you. Maybe it's me. I guess I'm afraid is all."

She grew excited again. "Of what? Why? Wait—don't tell me. Let me guess. I know!" She pointed at his mother. "She throws you in!"

He frowned. "No," he said. "Have you ever seen her do that? She doesn't do that."

"Oh, okay. Well, want my kickboard?" She handed him the board. "It's fun. Take it! C'mon!"

He pushed it away. "Isn't your dad supposed to be watching you? Where is he?"

She rolled her eyes. "He's *there*, next to your mom. See?"

He shrugged. "Oh, okay. I see."

"Your mom's pretty," she said.

He shrugged again. "Sure."

"How come I never see you in the water? Don't you know how to swim?" she asked again. This time, she threw the board into the pool. "See? It floats!"

He was unamused. "Want to learn something interesting?" he asked, trying to change the subject. "I can tell you exactly how high the water is from *there*. It's four feet and three inches. Want to know how I know?"

She shook her head. "No."

This frustrated him. Why was she bothering him if she didn't want to know what he was doing? "Why can't you just leave me alone? I don't feel like talking."

She went to retrieve the board.

"Hold on. Wait a minute." He perked as a new idea came to him. "Don't go. I have a question. How come?"

"How come what?" she said.

"How come it floats?"

"Why do you want to know—wait, I think I know. I think it's because; well, I guess ..." She scrunched her forehead deep in thought. "I don't know how come," she said with a big smile, as she waved a finger in the air. "But I'm going to find out!"

And with that question tickling the two of them, she skedaddled over to her father, who was sitting in a plastic white lounge chair with his head tucked into the newspaper.

Shoving the paper aside with her sopping wet hands, she climbed eagerly into his lap.

Her father looked down at the running black ink on his new white shorts. "What's up?"

She pointed to the board. "My friend wants to know why it doesn't drown."

"That's a good question, Ladybug, an excellent question," he answered. "She must be a highly intelligent friend."

Sam's mom, a pretty woman with high cheekbones, a slender nose, pale freckled skin, black sunglasses, and supple lips, chimed in from the neighboring lounge chair. "The *she* you are referring to is a *he,* and *he's* my son, Sam, thank you very much."

"Oh, I'm sorry. I thought, because of his voice, he was a gir—" Jack stopped himself from continuing the insult. "I'm Jack, Jack Zar. And you are?"

"Never mind," said Sophie, the woman. "It's not important." Glowering, she turned away.

Lanna shook her head. "No, Daddy! That's *Sophie* and that's *Sam.* Don't you know who they are by now? *I do.* I know them. I know everyone here. Just ask me next time."

"Sorry, Ladybug," he winked. "My mistake. Will do. Now, what was it that you asked me? Oh, that's right. *Why doesn't it drown?* What a powerful question. Let me think of how best to explain it to you. Correction, *to Sam.*" He paused until the words came to him. "You see, Lanna, the water is like a friend; it wants to help. It *wants* you to float. It *doesn't want* you to drown." He flipped his hands open and they both looked closely at the wisdom lines on his palms. "At the same time, and it's quite difficult to see it from here, if we were to look closely under my magnifying glass, the way we sometimes do together for fun when we're looking to see how much gunk you've gotten under your little fingernails, we'd see that your kickboard has space inside of it. The space inside is what allows the water to help. Does that make sense?"

"Uh, yeah," Lanna nodded, then stuck her tongue out and crossed her eyes in a playful jest.

"Okay, I forgive you, you guys are pretty funny," Sophie chimed in again, this time more gaily. "Your daughter's a q-tee-pie. How old is she?"

"Almost six," said Jack, and he returned the compliment. "Your son is rather smart for his age, wouldn't you say? How old is he?"

She pulled a mirror from her purse and reapplied her pink lipstick. "Too smart and too young."

From a distance, Sam signaled that he had grown impatient waiting for Lanna and he threw the kickboard into the pool rather gruffly, which caught Jack by surprise.

"Wow, Sophie, I can see your son's eyes from here. Are they made of cobalt? I'm surprised I didn't notice them sooner. I usually do notice things like this. You see, I'm a very observant man. Did he get his eyes from you? My, you're a lucky woman."

"I'm afraid he did not," she replied tartly. "Yep, you figured it out. Lucky me." She quickly reached for her smokes and shrunk back into her lounge chair.

"I'm sorry again," he responded. "That's twice now today that I've offended you. What color are *your* eyes? I bet they're stunning."

She lit her cigarette, and watching the orange embers flicker at the end of it, blew out a variety of smoke rings. Finally, she said, "You don't want to know what color my eyes are, *Jack Zar*. You want what's between my legs."

"That's where you're wrong, Sophie," he replied. "What's between your legs has nothing to do with your eyes. Let me make this clear to you: If you were my wife, I'd want you to know that your eyes are what make you special because, and this is important, because they belong to you. Because they are the windows through which you experience the world, and that perspective is what I'd love about *you*—I mean, *my wife*. That's what I love about my wife. And all people. And that is why I asked what color your eyes are. Right, Ladybug?"

***

That day, I nodded "right" to my father's question, though I didn't know why I was nodding.

I remember Sophie blushing and saying something along the lines of, "Well, I can see your daughter gets her good looks from your wife."

And my father saying back, "Just as I suspected; attractive and *intelligent*. So why the sour mood?"

And her saying to me, "Can you keep a secret?" and then sliding her glasses down her nose.

That's what startled me. "No, I don't like secrets," I said, and I galloped as fast and as far as I could from her black eye so that I could retrieve my kickboard.

CHAPTER FOUR

"WHY DOESN'T IT DROWN?"

When I returned to Sam, he asked, *"Well? Why doesn't it drown?* Took you long enough."

"Oh, yeah." I stopped and remembered. "It's something about the water; it, um, wants to help."

He frowned and furrowed his brows. "Did you even ask?"

"Yu-huh. I did. I did ask. He said it was like a friend."

"Like a friend? How?"

"It's like, when you want a friend, you get a friend, and then you can float. *Okay?*"

"You're saying the board and the water are friends?"

"Yeah. Daddy said if you look under the microscope, you see your friends."

"Like a mirror?"

"I don't know." I held my hands out to him. "Yeah, yeah, something like that. C'mon, Sam! Take my hand. I wanna show you how I do it in the deep end!"

He hesitated, and then took hold of my hands. "Okay. Fine. That makes sense. That's probably why you can see your reflection in the pool. Wait." He stopped again. "But what if I drown? You have to save me. You'll save me, right?"

"Don't worry," I said. "I won't let you drown. Promise."

He held out his pinky. "Swear?"

I crossed my pinky over his. "Swear."

That night, I told Mary about the bruise I had seen on Sam's mother's face, and she made me promise never to go over to his house. I asked her why, and told her that he'd never invite me anyway because I was a girl. Then I told her, "I get little bruises all the time. It's no big deal," but I knew in my heart that Sophie's were different.

"There are some things you're just too young to understand, Ladybug," she replied.

"Can I still play with him at the pool?"

"I wouldn't," she said.

But I did; I played. I played for weeks. I played until the Moon turned blue.

CHAPTER FIVE

THE KISS OF A BLACK SPIDER

Jack and Sam both jolted awake. Jack woke on the floor of his school's barren laboratory to the kiss of a black spider tiptoeing across his white overcoat. Sam woke in his ivy-laced lakefront chalet in his racecar-shaped bed to the sound of two consecutive—were they gunshots? Or had a car crashed? He didn't know; he had never heard either. Then, chirping crickets. Alone, both sat up and gazed out at the glowing blue Moon, tied together by an eerie sense of anticipation and the dizzying sensation of a permanent extraction, like sitting in the dentist's chair to have a filling replaced, only to find out that your tooth is fine, but your liver has been removed.

"Mom?" Sam called out. "Dad?" After waking from the noise, he climbed down the stairs to see if he could find his parents. He hoped his father wouldn't make fun of him again for waking up in the middle of the night "like a girl," which embarrassed him. His mother still let him sleep beside her at times, even if it meant she didn't sleep at all, and at school, the older children, who never slept with their parents, had shamed him for sleeping with her, but he couldn't help it. The dark terrified him. Why? He didn't know.

In his parents' room, he found two angels, or two demons—he would never quite be sure—toppled over one another on the beige-carpeted floor. His mother lay on her back with her see-through gray silk nightgown torn open down the middle. The sheets from their bed had been knotted, and splattered with red ink.

His father was naked, facedown, on top of her. Pillows were scattered everywhere around them. He held a filled-out credit card application in his hands. The details, Sam would later learn, were in his mother's name.

Sam turned off the bedroom lights, went to the window, stared up at the blue Moon, and returned to his mother on the floor in the dark. He pulled his father's body off of her. It fell to the floor with a thud. He kneeled beside her. "Are you there?" he whispered, and kissed her lips, then ran his fingers through her wavy hair, stumbling at a bald spot, where her hair had been pulled from her head and somehow tied to the metal feet of the bed. His heart beat fast and heavy. He held her limp hand to his pounding chest. He drew it to his own cheek and lay his head down upon her exposed wet breasts. She was still warm as he memorized her skin with his fingers. She still smelled of clove cigarettes, peach lotion, and red wine.

The phone rang. Over and over and over it rang. He froze. The crickets chirped. They chirped and chirped and chirped, and the sound of them chirping seemed to grow louder and louder, until all he could hear were their screams in his head, and just as he thought he couldn't take it anymore, and that his chest would explode from fear, the wooing of police sirens cut through the chirping. Their blue and red lights shone through the bay window onto the blood, onto her hair, onto more blood, onto more hair, until finally they stopped over his father's icy, contracted eyes—those eyes that everyone said were just like his.

"I'm sorry, Son," said one of the policemen. "They're dead."

The light never seemed so much worse than the dark.

CHAPTER SIX

"A WORD OF ADVICE, KID"

That night I startled awake to the sound of the door slamming. I climbed down from my loft bed to grab a glass of water and to see what all the commotion was about. As I slid to the door in my pajamas, the floorboards creaked. I poked my head into the hallway and into the kitchen. The lights were on.

As I was about to enter, I heard rubber boots squeak against the linoleum in our kitchen, and immediately retreated.

There were two police officers in our kitchen. One was pacing back and forth. He was speaking with my mother about something, someone; I couldn't quite make out his words—*the whereabouts of Father?*

The other was taking notes. He casually strutted toward the kitchen door and into the hall. I ducked behind my door so he wouldn't see me. He turned back into the kitchen and began talking into his walkie-talkie. "I don't think it's a double suicide. Over."

I shivered from the cold of being outside of my warm blankets but more so from the word "suicide," which was something we weren't supposed to ever talk *or even think* about, according to Mary.

Mary poked her face out from her bedroom. "Pssst, Ladybug, come here," she whispered, and pulled me into her bedroom by the hood of my sweatshirt. "Follow me," she instructed.

I did as I was told and followed. Except for a dim nightlight that was shaped like a butterfly, her room was dark.

"What's happening? What are we doing?" I asked. We walked past the dolls that she had strategically placed around a tea-party table set.

"Shh. You don't want them to hear you." She climbed to the top of her bed, stepped onto her dresser, and opened the window. "Come on," she said, as rain splattered against the windowsill and onto our box of Monopoly. "We have to get out of here. It's not safe."

I climbed beside her onto the dresser. The wind blew, and the leaves and the branches of the trees crashed harshly against each other. She threw her backpack over the side of the window. We dangled our legs over the sill, took a deep breath, and holding hands, "1-2-3," we jumped.

The grass was wet. I slipped and my bones landed hard against the dirt. My fleece pants became soaked to the ankle with water.

"Come on. Up you go." Mary helped me up. "Now, run!" she said. "Let's race! On your mark, get set, go!"

We raced past the cottage, opposite the trail to the cavern, away from the pines and the oaks, through the wet and windy moonlit night, until we reached the ladder to our neighbor's tree house. I plowed up ahead of Mary, shoving her aside, until I reached the top.

Victorious, that's when I heard—no, felt—a vibration that I had only come to know through instinct. I looked down, scanning everywhere below me. There was Mary. She had slipped, and her shoulder was contorted in such a way that I knew something rotten had happened.

"Mary? Are you okay?" I climbed ferociously back down.

"Mary? Are you okay?" I repeated, this time more afraid, as I stood over her body.

She didn't speak. I didn't know what to do, so I kicked the mud away from her arms, got down beside her, and held her until finally she let out a cry. "Lanna, get help. Get help. Help!"

"Okay!" I got back up, feeling foolish, and ran as fast as I could to the cottage, where I knocked on the door to get back inside, but the wind crashed harder than it had before—no one could hear my knocking. I tried to climb back in through the window, but it was too high. I grabbed a pebble and threw it through the open window in Mary's bedroom, hoping the noise would draw Mother's attention away from the officers in the kitchen and over to me. The rock hit the glass, and some of it ricocheted into my face.

No one heard. No one came. The rain pounded.

Defeated, I ran to the edge of the dirt road—a half mile from our cottage—even farther from the tree house. I stood along the outskirt, water penetrating every part of my body, hoping someone would see me as they drove by. If I had to, I planned to jump out into the road—the drivers would have to notice.

The police caught me in their lights coming down the road. "My sister is hurt." The rain pounded. "I need help. Help me!" I hollered.

One officer ran back down the road to the cottage to get Mother, while the other pulled me into his vehicle and, with my instruction, he drove us to Mary. When we reached her, the neighbors were already outside and had called an ambulance. Mary had fallen and landed on a toy that pierced through her and dislocated her shoulder. We had to leave the toy stuck inside her arm; we were told it was safer to have a surgeon remove it properly. I wanted to ride in the emergency car, but Mother said I would be too upset.

"Can Lanna please ride with you two?" Mother asked, as she climbed into the emergency vehicle with Mary.

The officer with curly black hair that looked sort of like mine took me by the hand and strapped a seat belt around me in the front seat. He gave me his hat and put his police coat around me.

"Don't worry," he said. "She'll be okay."

I said nothing the entire ride.

My father arrived at the hospital shortly afterward. I was so glad to see him, but my mother was furious. "Why didn't you tell me, Jack? How could you do this to me? You did this to us. This happened because of you! Because of you!" She began hitting him as though he had done something awful, the worst thing a person could do.

"Ma'am," said the officer who had put his coat around me. "Can I give you a minute with your husband? I'd like to speak with your daughter alone. Is that all right with you? You can watch from there." He pointed to a table in the cafeteria.

Mother looked at Father, and he nodded.

"Mama." I pulled her sleeve. "I don't want to. I want to be with Mary."

"Don't worry, Lanna. The doctor is taking care of Mary right now," she said. "Just answer the officer's questions. Then you can see Mary." She rose with my father, who seemed to shrink as he dragged himself behind her. "We'll be around the corner there." The two of them went over to the table next to the vending machines. Father held Mother as she cried. I could hear her say, "You did this to us, Jack. You did this. We're never going to get through this. You did this to us. Why did you do this?"

The officer sat beside me. "Are you hungry?"

I wasn't. I was sick to my stomach. "No," I said. He handed me a pretzel.

"You seem like a smart girl; a good one, too, the way you helped your sister like that. You know, it could've been a lot worse."

I sat silently.

"Why were you two running away?" he asked.

"I don't know," I told him. "I was scared."

"What scared you?"

"I heard the door slam, and I saw your boots. Teacher Molly at school says the police are there to protect you."

"And that made you afraid?"

I nodded timidly. "If the police are there to protect you, then they must be coming to protect you from someone." I gleaned his reaction. "Right?"

He smiled. "Right. So you were afraid someone was coming? Who did you think it was?"

I quieted.

After a minute, he handed me another pretzel. "How'd you get that scrape below your eye?" he asked. "You have a little bruise there, too. Mind if I take a closer look?" He looked me in the eye and lifted my chin. "Does it sting?"

"No," I told him.

He tore open a little packet that held a cloth soaked in alcohol. "It's a wipe for your face," he said. "I'm going to clean the blood off, all right?"

"All right," I said, and hesitated. "I think I cut myself when I threw the rock at Mary's window." He lifted my chin and gently ran the wipe over my cheek where the glass had entered my skin.

"Was it your father?" he asked.

"What do you mean?"

"Did your father hurt you?"

"No. Why would Daddy hurt me?" I replied, my face still in his hands.

"What if I asked you again, with your parents standing farther away? Would your answer be the same?"

"Why would it be different?"

"Okay, good," he said, nodding approvingly. "A word of advice, kid." He set down the wipe and handed me another pretzel. "I'm not saying there is going to be anything wrong with you, but in case there is, talk to someone. Someone you trust."

"Why would there be something wrong with me?" I asked.

"I'm not saying there will be," he said again. "But a lot of people will think there is. It might make you change your mind. Who do you trust, other than your mom and dad?"

"I trust Mary," I told him.

"Other than Mary. Anyone else?"

I pondered this. "Well," I told him, smiling, "I trust Grandpa. And Grandma too."

"Someone outside the family," he snapped. "A friend!"

I silenced. After a minute, I said, "I trust my friend—my friend Sam."

He handed me a pretzel. "Tell me about Sam."

I chewed. "Well, he says he's not supposed to be friends with girls, but he's my friend anyhow. I showed him how to use the kickboard. He's good at it now. He likes math *a lot*, but sometimes he's quiet."

"Really? Quiet about what?"

"I don't know," I said.

"Do you know his mom and dad?"

"His mom's really pretty," I told him. "She has red hair, and she smells good, and she smokes skinny cigarettes that smell like cinnamon or something like that."

"Can you tell me anything else about her?"

"Well," my stomach churned. "There is one thing. But I don't know if I should tell you. She said it was a secret."

"A secret?" he replied. "Go on."

I paused. I didn't know if it was right to tell.

After waiting, the officer said abruptly, "Listen, kid, I have some bad news for you. Sam's mommy is dead. She's in heaven now. If you care about Sam, you have to tell me her secret."

Shivers ran down my body. "I'm going to throw up!" I blurted. And then I did, right into the officer's lap.

After ten minutes or so of everyone around us shuffling to help us both get cleaned up, I slurped down a can of ginger ale and uneasily told the officer everything I knew.

No amount of makeup would ever conceal the swelling of Sophie's bruise from my memory.

Later, I climbed into Mary's hospital bed, and promised her that she could have all the Jell-O she wanted, even mine, as long as we never raced each other ever again. She agreed.

CHAPTER SEVEN

THE CHESTNUT REPORTER

June 22, 1988 | *The Chestnut Reporter* **|
Crime | E7**

A 40-year-old man from the nearby town of
Chestnut, New Jersey, was arrested Tuesday
for the alleged murder of husband and wife
Nico and Sophie Azurite. The man was
apprehended in his home, several blocks
from the scene of the crime, where neighbors
say they could hear him arguing with his
family. The suspect is also facing allegations
of domestic abuse.

MISSWIRED by Tara Makhmali

September 18, 1989 | *The Chestnut Reporter* **| Local | A5**

One year after the grisly death of Nico and Sophie Azurite, Jack Zar has been sentenced to 15 years in prison. The verdict comes as a surprise. Local opinion on the outcome of the Azurite case remains conflicted:

"I've known Jack a long time. This is inconsistent with his personality. He cared deeply for people. Something isn't right."
—Wu Lee, College Student

"I don't know if Jack did this crime; I didn't see him much, but I always suspected he was capable. He was a weird guy, always scribbling pictures of mold into his notebook. Mold? Who likes mold? Heck, I'd seen the way he looked at Nico's wife, always trying to help her and such. If he was trying to help my lady that way, I'd show him a thing or two, weird as he was, that's for sure."
—James Stevens Frank, Restaurant Owner

"Nico killed Sophie long before Jack ever could."
—Gin Su, Neighbor of Deceased Couple

"A man at odds with his own soul suffers, regardless of his earthly punishment. Whether justice is with or against him is only as relevant as his ability to repair and heal his suffering soul."
—Andrew "Handy" Yates Oates, Philanthropist Billionaire

"The DA is sending a blunt message to citizens that violators of the Gun Law Safety Act will be punished without mercy, regardless of who they are or what their good intentions. If Mr. Zar had used common sense to notify the authorities, Nico and Sophie would be alive today. This is what happens when citizens take law enforcement into their own hands."

—John Kelper, Partner Kazath Law, Politician

"They're wrong. Jack's a nerd with a big heart. So he gave her a gun to protect herself. So what? That doesn't make him a killer. You ever meet Sophie? There wasn't a man in town that wasn't curious about that woman. Jack's only mistake was that his intrigue naturally led him toward the things no one ever wants to look more closely at. This wasn't his fault. He's a martyr, not a criminal."

—Moz Zane, Neighbor of Zar Family

CHAPTER EIGHT

"YOU GOT TALENT, SUGAR"

Two weeks after my sixth birthday, Mother, Mary, and I walked my father through the gravel, past the prison's barbed-wire entrance gate. Mother wore a black lace mid-length dress that hugged her hips, pearl earrings, wine-stained lipstick (or maybe it was just wine; I couldn't tell), sunglasses that said *Dior* across the side of them, and a large black hat that tilted to one side and was covered with fake yellow sunflowers. She looked hollow, as though someone had stolen something from her that she could never get back and somehow she was making up for the loss by wearing her fanciest clothes.

I wore my only pink dress, two clips to hold back the black curlies that kept sweeping across my left eye, and a pair of black Converse sneakers, which I wanted Mary to wear too, since we both owned a pair and I liked the feeling of being part of Mary's team. She did not share the same sentiment. It frustrated her that Mother always dressed us as twins, and while we all waited in the car for Mary to return from the bathroom, she quickly changed out of her pink dress into navy slacks, a white ruffled shirt, red high heels, and one of my father's ties fashioned around her neck like a bow, which somehow made her look as though she had boobs. I couldn't understand why she would want them. Mother always complained that hers were hurting her back.

A patrol officer from the county prison winked at us and catcalled my mother on the way past. My father glared at him as though he wanted to burn a hole through his head. "Come here, you two," he said, as crisply as I had ever heard him speak, and we jumped to it.

He kissed Mary and me each on the forehead and pulled us close. My mother held her hand to her mouth and whimpered sorrowful I-love-you's.

I pushed my father away. "You did this to us, Jack," I said to him, my heart and words hardened by the sound of Mother's desperation.

Mother pulled me to her and cradled me in her arms. Sternly, she said, "No, sweetheart, he didn't. He loves us."

Mary wrapped herself around my father and begged to go into prison with him. "Please, can I come with you, Daddy? Please. Why can't I live with you in prison?" she uttered over and over, while my father stood completely frozen and expressionless, as though paralyzed. Once Mother finally had enough of listening to Mary squeal, she pulled my sister off of my father with one hand, grabbed my hand with the other—I still remember that she had the softest hands—and she dragged us both back into the beat-up gray Volvo that my father used to get himself to and from campus every day, our only mode of transport.

"There's no turning back," Mother said sternly. "We have to be strong for each other. That's all we can do."

And like a whisper that never had a chance to make its way out of my lips, my father was gone. He had checked himself into prison. And right then and there, I resolved never to see him again. The words *"You did this to us, Jack"* spun in my head as though they could remedy his vacancy from my life.

Afterward, we drove to a church two hours from home. My mother, who had never before expressed an interest in religion, went into a confessional, while Mary and I waited in the empty pews, flipping through pages of a gold-leafed Bible and wondering why anyone would ever want to read it, when a black woman (probably in her late twenties) with shimmery green eyes, rosy cheeks, and braided hair, wearing a cowboy hat, a purple sash, and dangling chandelier earrings, sat down next to us with a sketch pad and a box filled with colored pencils.

"Why are you here, children?" She grinned. "Goofing off from school?"

"Why are *you* here?" I retorted.

She flipped open her sketchpad. "To draw, of course. See?" She flipped through her pad to show me her sketches of the stage. "See how the light comes in through the stained glass behind the podium there? Isn't it beautiful?"

"I don't think it's beautiful," I said. "I think it's ugly. But I like your hat."

"Oh yeah? How so?" She cocked her head. "Thanks. I borrowed it from the handyman."

"I don't know," I told her. "I can't explain it."

"Okay, smarty-pants," she said. "So show me." And she handed me her pad and her pencils.

I stared at the page. "It's like this," I showed her, smudging the yellow into the black, the orange into the purple, the blue into the green, and then running my eraser through it in circles. "The light hits like that, but then you see it like this."

She leaned in. After a few seconds, she leaned back. "Shoot, you got talent, Sugar!" She snapped her fingers. "Anyone ever tell you that? Why don't you keep working on that while I work out some other things."

She winked, rose from the pew, strutted over to a grand piano, slid out the piano bench (which echoed as it skid against the floor), and sat down. "Ready for this, babies? Tell me if you think Mama's got it right." She smiled, and her fingers began gliding up and down the piano as though they were satin and the keys were skin. Vibrating and bouncing from wall to cavernous wall through the rainbow of stained glass, the most melodic hymn I had ever heard poured out from her belly. It was as though she had lifted me out of my body and had taught me to fly. I closed my eyes, obeyed the music, and let the colored pencils carry me away to wherever they told me to be on the page. When she finished singing, I looked at Mary, who was busy redlining the Bible. "These passages don't make much sense to me," she said. "I'd like clarity here."

I looked back down at the coloring pad, not at all interested in Mary's amendments to the Bible.

"You didn't make that sketch, did you?" she asked, with a bit of surprise in her voice.

"I don't know," I told her. "I think I did."

"Holy crap. I mean—oops! You have to show Mom! It'll brighten her day."

***

It's hard to believe that life carried on after Jack went to prison, but it did. Art became my salvation, my very reason for existing. I started with pencils and eventually moved on to anything I could get my hands on. Acrylics. Pottery. Photography. Graphic design. Wherever the melodies transported me.

But as the calendar turned the days into months, and the seasons revolved into years, I couldn't help but hold on to these two divergent, and yet inexplicably linked, memories— the stunted goodbye of my expressionless father as my mother dragged Mary and me away from the prison; and the vivacious hymn that walked through my walls, lifting me out of my body, filling my anger with sublime creativity, and using me as its vessel to produce whatever it wanted from me. The question of why God—or consciousness, as my father had taught me—had linked these two, to use his words, "divergent and bimodal," moments together, I came to experience as my life's defining struggle. And this obvious dichotomy enabled the already growing cloud of speculation over how well I would, and was, adjusting to the inescapable fact that *I was the daughter of a criminal,* which shot me spinning into a cyclone of confusing advice from social workers, guidance counselors, psychiatrists, and well-meaning savants, all of whom wanted to make sure I'd be okay, but whose prose dimmed my glow and muddied my ability to see who I was. Collectively, their refrain went something like this:

"Lanna, dear, your father is in prison. You're the daughter of a criminal. How do you feel about that? You have to know that, because of your father, people may not think highly of you. There were a lot of people in this town who respected Nico. I suppose they respected your father's academic achievements too. But you don't have to be like him. You can be like your mother. Is she still crying all the time? Well, you can be whoever you want to be, though you might want to reconsider running for public office, if that ever was an idea of yours. You might want to tone back your quirky behavior too. I recommend you stay away from the boys. Not ladylike. I know you're getting a lot of attention; we're just trying to keep you away from trouble. Also, a pretty girl such as yourself, well, you're going to have a lot of eyes on you. Probably should stop all that dancing about; we don't want to see you hanging naked from the stripper poles—that is common for girls without fathers, you know. Oh, and one last thing. Be careful of making art that is too dark; people will think you are one of those weird girls who cuts themselves. Where's your smile? Now, smile; *smile for the camera!*"

Suddenly it seemed that all eyes were on me. Not for me being the girl I remembered being, but for another character whom I had never before met. A character who was quiet and contained, gifted and alone, and whose value was overshadowed by a single snapshot in time.

How disconnected I had grown from the life I once knew, from the self I once knew. I suppose, in hindsight, one never recalls what it means to be oneself when you are free to be whoever it is that you are and want to be. Existential thought isn't necessary, since you are too busy being you. Unforgivably, the tides of life had carved me a new path. I was the star of a rerun about an absentee father and his soon-to-be-screwed-up daughter. My new role was to please the educators, gossipers, worriers, analysts, and even well-meaning friends, whose words were, "You're a good girl," but whose eyes said, "We're waiting for you to f*ck up your life," and that meant, "Lanna, you'd better be perfect. Tick. Tock."

PART TWO

PART TWO

CHAPTER NINE

LANNA: TWENTY YEARS LATER

"Don't be such a perfectionist, Lanna. Keep your head down. Do your work. You're speaking out of turn. Things are the way they are around here because that's the way they are, the way they always have been. One day, it'll be your turn to tell people what to do. You can ask as many questions as you want then."

These were the pearls of wisdom from my nervous self-proclaimed supervisor, a man frustrated by my very presence on the planet. I stared at his nose as he spoke, nodding my head at regular cross-eyed intervals so as to appear attentive. I couldn't help but feel he would get along great with my asshole boyfriend, another man who couldn't spend enough time telling me I wasn't operating at the "right level." I could see them sitting together at the bar now, a pair of giant douchebags boasting about how silly and imperfect I was, jeering about how every pathetic thing they'd ever done in their entire lives was better than anything I had ever done.

"Yes, fine." I nodded. "Understood." I grabbed my sketches from the display aisle, along with my notes, and let my *superior* male equal do the remainder of the talking.

"So you see, Tom," he said, waving his arms in the air, ceasing his arm gestures only to sculpt his gelled, Mohawk-styled hairdo. "We're going to skim the banner and modify the J2 files, so that the digital barrier of the AQM demystifies the customer while we capture their EQ impressions into our DM, which will forecast all of their buying patterns and lead to high sales."

And as the client began to look justifiably confused by the made-up tech terms, he threw this saucy phrase into the mix: "In other words, it's the Uber meets Red Bull of ROI."

What a load of ... I held back laughter over the phony, over-used Uber analogy.

The client was impressed. The parties shook hands. The meeting ended.

Swindled another one, I thought, and we swung through the glass doors of the conference room out into the artists' studio, where I briefly considered hanging myself.

It was the same story we'd been spitting out ever since I had joined the agency as a zesty twenty-two-year-old. Seven years dedicated to this palace of bullshit, and I couldn't get out of the meetings fast enough.

Of course, at some mind-illuminating juncture, the once-glowing client would dissolve our contract for lack of transparency and blatant over-billing, stemming mostly from our inability to manage the heaps of bodies we threw at their projects. It was as much their fault as it was our own ... "100 women can't make a baby in one month," the saying goes, though in their slimy world, money could solve any problem. And so it went. And so we took advantage of it. And as long as I got to wear my signature red-soled Christian Louboutin stilettos and could occasionally tend to my creative desires, I was fine. Just fine.

I was not fine. I was far from fine. My enchantment with the prestige of ad agency life—modular furniture, bright walls, plasma televisions, neon lights, and the stupid Ping-Pong table no one ever used, for lack of time and fear of being fired—had faded considerably. I was so ready to flee the MBA corporate double-speak world I inhabited nearly every waking hour of my life. It seemed so far from the reason I had fallen in love with art in the first place.

And, yet, like an old familiar blanket, I grasped on to the reverie of fringe benefits that the lifestyle afforded: a carousel of iconic dance parties to keep me drunk, twirling, and laughing; attractive twenty-something working teams that kept me sexually aroused while I crafted; and a *pro bono* anti-smoking campaign that allowed me to trick myself into believing I, solely, was responsible for saving lives. These illusions of a life worth living, though fun, made me hate myself.

But the other true benefit, if one could call it that, was the perception that my ambitious banker boyfriend had of my affiliation to the prestigious ad agency. He viewed the company as single-handedly upgrading my personal status, bringing me up to "his level." This view, which he frequently espoused in our shared 500-square-foot one-bedroom condo, with the combination of prestige and working unsustainably long hours, in his supreme eyes, elevated me in a way that apparently nothing else could. I ignored the feeling that his words, his presence, even, added to my depression. I needed to feel as though I were succeeding, even if that meant settling for a man who constantly belittled me.

Yes, I worked for liars and cheaters, and I created art that made more liars and more cheaters; and yes, the prestige, or façade, for that matter, made me seesaw between laughing and drunk and deeply disturbed, but if I were ever going to find a way out of this horrible relationship, I knew I needed to suck it up, to put my head down, to keep working so I could make enough money to afford my own abode. And at least I was being recognized for something other than being a screw-up.

"Look at me," I told myself. "I had a messed-up upbringing, but I beat the odds! See? I am a real winner."

***

The questions started as soon as I entered the apartment. He grabbed my arm—not the embrace of a missed lover, but an Indian burn.

"Where were you?" he asked.

"I told you I was stopping at the farmers' market in Union Square with Heidi after work. Let go of my arm."

"I don't believe you. What do you have in those bags?"

I wanted to say, *why would I lie about going to a f*cking farmers' market, you douche*, but instead, I tried to pull my arm away. "Let go of my arm," I said. Unmoved, his fingernails embedded themselves deeper into my skin. I inhaled to the sting and released my breath. "Look, it's just fruit, okay? I picked up the Asian pears you like. See? I'm going to put these groceries in the fridge."

"Heidi's a slut. You shouldn't hang out with her. I didn't know they were *Asian* pears; I don't like them anymore."

"You don't? Why not? Please don't call her that. She's the nicest friend I have. C'mon, please let go of my arm." I shuddered again to the rippling bite of his pointers in my bicep and tried to pull my body away.

He held on. "If you were *at my level,* you wouldn't be seen with her. You know Asians are not *at my level* either. Don't you care about your reputation? Not everyone is as forgiving as I am about your past."

F*cking racist piece of shit, I thought. "Okay, I get it; no Heidi, no Asian pears. I'm sorry. Can I please put these away now?"

He released my arm, and I sighed.

"Do you even care about me?" he asked.

No. I don't. I am terrified of you, I wanted to say, but instead, I said, "Of course I do; that's why I got you the pears." I smiled, while on the inside screaming. "How can you even ask me that?"

"If you cared about me, you wouldn't go to the market with Heidi."

"Well, what am I supposed to tell her? She says she's worried about me. She thinks something is wrong."

"Why would she think that? Did you tell her something you didn't tell me? Forget it. Just tell her that you need to focus on your work so that you can be *at my level.* She'll understand. If you care about me, that's what you'll do. Anyway, would she even hang out with you if she knew about your dad? I doubt it."

"Okay," I said. "You're right." I held back tears, put the pears away, closed the door to the bedroom, popped in my headphones, and grabbed my pencils.

CHAPTER TEN

SAM: TWENTY YEARS LATER

"From Rags to Riches: The Orphaned Billionaire Who Caught the Wall Street Whale," read *Elite Investor*'s feature page.

How Sam had grown into such a big shot, he didn't know. He smirked a pearly smirk. He knew a little.

The villa was a swift car ride away. Correction, a bumpy car ride. The driver didn't speak much English, and yet, somehow he read Sam like a book. *"Para ti,"* he said, lowering the windows and handing Sam a 7UP in a green glass bottle, along with a miniature bottle of dark rum.

The heat of the blazing sun, coupled with the hiccups of island roadways, had a way of spoiling a vacation before Sam had a chance to enjoy it. He always traveled by way of *Rafael's Luxury Car Service*, which in reality was a decaying yellow cab with a busted A/C, ripped interior seats, no seat belts, and a large trunk with the number "8" spray-painted in large bubbly letters on the back of it. Drinking and driving was legal on the island, and, in fact, encouraged. Sam liked this, except that he wasn't very good at it, which he had learned from experience back home.

He had at one point paid to transport his mint Jaguar convertible to the tropical island by boat from Manhattan— the center of the universe—but it never made it to the villa because the boat had sunk. *Rafael's Luxury Car Service* was consistent. Always on time. Always friendly. And, most importantly, always sober and able to avoid street trouble.

Now that his Wall Street conquests had made headlines and his seat at the Connecticut AG hedge fund had gone public, it was time to dodge the media. The fact that he had broken his ironclad non-compete and gotten away with it heightened interest like static on a pair of ladies' Spanx. Of course, the mandatory audit forcing him to relinquish his files and devices to a team of dorky, cross-eyed investigators left him no other choice but to take refuge at one of his multiple *pieds-à-terre*.

The cab stopped. The driver stepped out, wiped the sweat from his own forehead, adjusted his olive-green trousers, and rounded the corner to open Sam's door.

"That's not necessary," Sam said, exiting the cab as swiftly as he had entered. "I am capable of opening doors," he announced, eager to imbibe the fresh sea air.

A breeze blew in off the water. He inhaled the clear air, pleased to see that the pink flowers draping over the planters that lined his villa had been well pruned. The flamingos in the yard appeared content, too. One was darting its head into the pond for fish; another was asleep, her long neck and pointy head nestled into her chest as she stood on one leg.

The driver casually rounded to the back of the car to open the trunk.

"Thank you." Sam handed him a twenty and began rolling his J.W. Hulme Co. leather luggage up the walkway to the entrance. "Stay close," he continued. "I have dinner plans at—" He paused. "*Comida en el pueblo.*"

The driver returned to his post on the cliff, popped his head back into the trunk, grabbed a green ukulele, and positioned himself comfortably on the hood of his vehicle.

"Hello? Anyone here?" Sam whistled. "Hello? Hello? Anyone here? Paloma? I'm here!" He rolled his luggage to the center of the marble foyer over the ship-wheel tile medallion in the floor. A passage door through the foyer opened slowly. Paloma, a hefty older woman with almond-shaped crow's-feet eyes; wiry black and silver hair, which she wore in an oily bun; and a cheeky smiling face that could melt your heart, wrapped her small, plump body around him.

Smothering his face against her drooping chest, she welcomed him with full force. "Mister Sam! Welcome!" she exclaimed exuberantly, squeezing him as though he were a lemon and she was making lemonade. "How was your flight?"

"Fine, thank you. Now that's enough hugging. There. There." He pushed away from her awkward, overbearing embrace, and corrected his bangs. "Good to see you too. But now, if you don't mind, I have work to do."

"But Mister Sam." She appeared offended. "Your breakfast is ready, just the way you like. You cannot work on an empty stomach. Luís will carry your luggage upstairs. Come, come, come. Come with me."

"I'd like to settle in first," he said, rolling his luggage to the wrought-iron rail and bouncing it up the stairs.

"Mister Sam!" she insisted, pacing rapidly behind him. "Breakfast first! Leave the bag for Luís! I've been cooking all morning. Please, I insist. Come. Follow me."

Upon noticing that she had acquired a limp since he had last seen her, Sam gave up and unlatched his fingers from the suitcase.

She recovered her breath as she hunched to set his luggage aside. *"Pendajo,"* she cursed.

Paloma never cleaned the house in the manner Sam preferred. The strain of housekeeping and tending to her five children, and their combined twenty grandchildren, had taken its toll on her body, particularly her lower back. There were cobwebs behind doors; the sheets were often still wet when you lay in them; and despite the villa's top-of-the-line appliances, she washed the dishes by hand. The laundry, which she often dried along a clothes-wire since they frequently lost electricity, was often sacrificed to the volcanic mountains below, and sometimes Sam could see his favorite briefs washing away into the ocean as he sipped his scotch and gazed out over the balcony.

As Sam followed her through the French doors and out toward the veranda, Paloma kicked aside a heaping ball of hair that had collected at the corner with her black Reebok sneakers and contentiously roped the sheer white curtains away from the door. Finally, she pointed him toward the table, where breakfast was set.

"Here you are," she smiled widely, her eyes gleaming. "Fresh croissants, strawberries, poached eggs, French toast, pork sausage, avocados, fried plantains, mango, whipped butter, whipped cream, syrup, jam, coffee, grapefruit juice, and watermelon. All your favorites."

Steadily sliding the heavy white metal chair out for him, and tucking aside the lace table tapestries she had sewn in her spare time, she nodded politely for him to sit. "I hope you like it."

He smiled and looked down at his plate.

The air was dense. The poached eggs had hardened.

"This looks phenomenal," he said, inspecting the rest of the meal.

The watermelon was carved into the shape of a goldfish. He raised an eyebrow. Whenever Paloma's children needed favors, or when a lengthy list of repairs was looming, she always braced him with a full belly.

"Okay, Paloma, I'd rather know," he said. "Don't keep me waiting. What is it now? What needs fixing? Who needs my help?"

Sweat cascaded over his forehead. His stomach growled. "On second thought, can you please bring me a glass of ice water?" He unbuttoned his suit jacket, sat down, and placed an embroidered napkin carefully over his slacks.

She returned with a pitcher. "At least try to enjoy," she told him, and hurried away.

Her cooking had a tendency to make him think of life more favorably. His focus shifted.

Six months ago, a frail Asian headhunter from a *boutique* recruiting firm had pitched him a new employment opportunity, just as he had begun growing bored with his employer.

She boasted "exclusive client relationships" and "unparalleled opportunities," the way all the other recruiters did. But then she did something out of the ordinary; she sent him a living plant that emitted natural light, something he had never seen before in all of his time analyzing green investments. Its leaves were like solar panels, but the energy they stored emitted 2,000 lumens—extreme brightness for a plant whose leaves were no bigger than his thumb. She told him that AG had access to investments no one had ever heard of. "Imagine the unimaginable," she had said. "These are the types of innovations they have access to."

In spite of the sales gimmick, Sam was skeptical. He knew that the role and the sales version of the role always differed. He was well established in his successful career, and he had much to consider.

His first concern was the intention of AG's senior directors. Were they honest? What were their motivations? And, more importantly, *what were they hiding?*

Splash a big name across the newspaper precisely at the time of an unfolding bank scandal and the public is smitten with distraction. His story—the orphan who beat the odds to become a billionaire—could be public bait should the smarmy banking empire come unhinged and the American people take the hit. It was easier for laymen to believe that that same orphan-to-billionaire was fraught with shady dealings than it was for them to understand that a committee of seniors at multiple banks jointly approved complex, logically flawed high-risk investment strategies that took their homes and buried their families with debt. Sam would not allow himself to be a scapegoat. He had no intention of isolating himself more than he already had, and unlike many he knew, he felt responsible for maintaining a functioning economic system for the betterment of all.

So he did his due diligence. He hired private investigators. And, to his delight, the position was legitimate. For a delicious salary, and with many trusted colleagues expected to join, he accepted the position of chief investment officer for what he believed was a remarkable company. He would relish re-engineering AG toward further success.

There was another unspoken benefit to transitioning to the new position. Burying himself in work meant he didn't have to think about ...

Burying *her*.

As he sensed her, the essence of blood-iron and mint lip-gloss entered his mouth. He swore he could see her there, sitting next to him, walking through his walls, listening to him drone on and on about work, and gazing out into the horizon. Her shiny black hair. Her glowing golden complexion smiling into the water, staring out into the Caribbean Sea at the silvery shapes cast by the sun.

Nguyen.

He lost himself in the memory of her bulbous curves wading into the ocean. In the little cut on her upper lip from when she tripped over a conch shell. He lost himself in her slender upright form. Her perfectly tanned legs. The mole on her shoulder. The way her arms free-floated above her head and her pregnant belly protruded from her one-piece swimsuit. How she pranced *croisé devant* without a care in the world on the white sand. How she squealed with excitement upon finding clamshells and mussels, crabs and iguanas. How she pushed him to pay attention: *"What do you want, Sam? Are you present? Do you see the mountains? Do you see the dolphins bouncing in and out of the water? Do you see the neon fish? If you want this, if you want me, if you want our child, you have to get out of your head. Come, kiss me. Let me hold you."*

"More juice, Mister Sam?" Paloma returned with a carafe of freshly squeezed fruit juice.

Sam coughed. "Ahem. No, thank you." He rose from the table. He was disappointed in himself for allowing feelings to make him vulnerable again.

She fumbled for a moment. "Mister Sam, your room is not ready." She hesitated. "Go for a walk on the beach. Enjoy your vacation."

"No, thanks," he said, shaking his head.

"Mister Sam, please," she pleaded. "Take a walk to the sea. The sea misses you. Don't you miss the sea?"

"How long until it's ready?"

"Fifteen minutes."

"Okay," he sighed, softening. "No problem. Now, was there something else you wanted to tell me?"

"Yes," she said. "It's Vän. The nanny can't watch Vän anymore. She has to leave. Her husband is sick. We will need to find something for him to do."

"Can't Luís watch him?"

"No." She shook her head contritely. "If you may permit, is it possible he goes to the beach with you? He doesn't want Luís. *He wants his father.* He has been talking about you all week long. He loves you very much. It will make him happy to see you."

"Well," he paused. "I suppose I do have the time."

She continued. "Mister Sam, you know, permit me again. When my grandbabies were in *escuela* like Vän is now, they thought I was a superhero like in the comic books. These are the best days, Mister Sam. Don't let them slip."

"But Paloma," he grinned. "You are a superhero."

"Oh, stop it, Mister Sam. You know, you're the superhero. What you've done for me, for my family. The work you give us. Thank you for that. I'm old now. Soon you will want a younger maid."

Sam shook his head. "No, Paloma. I prefer things to remain exactly as they are. This is your home. Now, have you dressed Vän for the beach yet?"

She nodded, knowingly.

CHAPTER ELEVEN

KISS WITH A GAZE

In the distance, a bashful fox twirled about in the grass. It perked up at the sound of a crackling tree branch, and quickly returned to its more pressing demand of rubbing its hiney against the raspberry bushes. Mary had picked me up from the train station an hour southwest of Mother's cottage, after Heidi and a fledgling artist friend/coworker straight out of college who held a torch for me and for whom I held zero romantic interest helped pack what few belongings I owned from *his* flat in New York City in the middle of the night while *he* was away on business. It was an abnormally humid Thursday, even for the middle of May.

My sister had been visiting our mother once a month ever since starting college, and even as the youngest, and only, married female partner at her white-shoe law firm, she continued visiting Mom with fervor, come rain, shine, hell, or high water, and as anyone from New Jersey can tell you, this was no small feat, since it often rained so hard that sea levels would rise and black water would come slopping out of the ground, closing highways and suspending trains. If there was any consolation to the flooding, it was that Mother had inherited the anomalies of the cavern and its ecosystem, and when the water rose, she worked together with a litter of twinkly-eyed students to collect and label the brave flagellates that had journeyed into the basement pump from the cavern. Mary appreciated being witness to this spectacle—both of Mother's enjoyment (which was rare) and the even more rare glow-in-the-dark microbes in the basement, which she said reminded her that "anything with glow can be killed if not handled correctly," and that reminding herself of this made her a better leader to the younger lawyers at her firm.

I was not a good daughter. And I had not witnessed this marvel firsthand. I had visited merely a handful of times since graduating from high school, which was over a decade ago. After making the mistake of moving in too quickly with a man whom I hardly knew because of his résumé, and because, for some strange reason, the baritone in his voice made me orgasm twice as hard whenever I heard him speak; and because I had quickly realized how racist and dangerous he was, I was too embarrassed to visit Mother. I was too embarrassed to even call. I didn't want to expose her to him. But when I did, Mother was kind, as she always was, and relieved. "Darling," she told me on the telephone, "this isn't your fault. Come to me with these things. You're a very loving girl. It confuses you sometimes, the way it does your father."

Despite her kindness, I still couldn't help but cry the entire train ride home, still convinced that I had let my mother down by failing at life, and cringing at the idea of being anything like the father who had brought so many tears to her eyes. At the age of 29, which I felt was too old to be in this predicament, I was ashamed to be moving back home—even if it was only for a week or so, until I could figure out where to live next. I wanted everyone, especially my mother, to see how successful I was, but I had finally come to the terrible conclusion that there was no bigger failure in life than parading around as though I were some big shot, when the reality was the exact opposite. And this folly—pretending that my life was perfect—was giving my ex free rein to do whatever he wanted to whomever he wanted, whenever he wanted. "You aren't satisfying me sexually anymore," he told me in his slick, snarky voice a few days before I packed up my stuff. "Remember how we talked about you doing that thing? Obviously, if you gave me what they give me, I wouldn't need to cheat on you."

He made me sick. Everything that came out of his mouth made me sick, and I wanted to understand how I didn't see it sooner. *Was I that horny?* I couldn't stand being in that apartment for one more millisecond, even if it meant I had to suck it up and move back home with my mother—the person I wanted to impress more than anyone else in the world.

Stepping barefoot into the yard, raw from the overnight hustle, I surprised myself and giggled at the silly fox, whose failure to relieve its itch amused me. It also made me consider whether I should tell Mother not to collect the berries from the bottom branches.

Carrying a hot cup of coffee and my ex's original love letters (just so I could torture myself some more by dissecting his trap) through the grass, which was still moist from the morning dew, I strutted toward my favorite spot in the woods, threw my cardigan aside, removed a few sticks, and plopped into a cross-legged sitting position on a flat rock under my old favorite oak.

I had spent my childhood in these trees, hiding from peers and guidance counselors who wanted to box me in to their own screwed-up version of Little Miss Perfect. Now I didn't know whom I was hiding from.

Look at me, I thought. *Did they win? Did they get what they wanted? Little Miss Perfect is finally having the breakdown they were all rooting for.*

I settled into the warm breeze against my sticky skin. The trees always cheered me up. They were my haven. They didn't judge. They didn't seek to fix; they didn't see me as broken. They were calm in my company. I was calm in theirs.

Alone with my thoughts, I was free to be whoever I felt like being—whoever I *desired* being. An athletic girl. A creative girl. A caring girl. A dancing girl. A curious girl. A naughty woman. Even as the occasional tabloid reporter came snooping to gather opinions about my father's case, they were never able to rattle me here.

I broke out into a cold sweat. *If only I could find my balance now.*

The winds whooshed. The birds sensed my presence. Sometimes they sang an aria for me. Sometimes they entirely ignored me. No matter what they did, I belonged to them. Together and with one another, we were connected by the space that connects all things to Mother Earth, and Mother Earth to all things. Of course, to an onlooker, the abundance of such creatures would've been subtle, unconsciously ignored, and if spotted, reasoned as coincidence. If there was one thing I knew for sure, it was that everything in life had a pulse. Everything lived. Everything died. Everything was connected. Even when bad connections drove us to love unworthy people, we all belonged to the planet. Nature would take care of us. And I needed it to take care of me now.

I sat outside alone until the sun set, the glowing blue Moon shone onto the leaves of the oak, and all I could see was the small trail and a handful of pinecones leading back to the cottage. Mary appeared with a round flashlight and she convinced me to join her inside. "I want to spend as much time with you as I can before going back to work," she said, and reached to pull me up and out of my funk, as if that were even possible.

I let her walk me back inside, where she had lit a lavender-scented candle and had poured me a cup of chamomile tea. I went with it, even allowing her to tuck me into bed as though I were her little baby sister again.

My mind raced into the wee hours of the night, unable to soothe itself from the longing for true love, while the brutal springs of my distressed mattress, which I never ceased to complain about (even knowing how little money my mother had), dug brazenly into the sides of my body, making sleep both a nightmare and an act of desperation. Covered in perspiration, I finally gave up, sat up, and muscled open the window beside my bed.

Flecks of white paint peppered the air, and the screen was worse; it was coated in yellow and green pollen that made my allergies flare—the ones I had, surprisingly, acquired from living in the city for too long.

I grabbed a tissue, wiped my nose, and reread the love letter from my ex for the hundredth time. I wanted to dissect how he had put me under his spell, so that I could know to beware next time such a vulgar creature came for me. The first line was a quote by a 19th-century Spanish poet, Gustavo Adolfo Bécquer:

"The eyes, like windows to the soul, can kiss with a gaze."

Whoosh. I knew what had happened. I had gone blind with euphoria.

It continued, "I see you for who you are, and still I gaze. I love you, despite that secret of yours. Who else can see you that way? With that secret of yours—you know, the one that makes you feel weird."

I mumbled "idiot" into my pillow. *Would I ever stop seeing myself as the daughter of a criminal?* His words had always had a profound power over me, somehow obscuring my desire for hopeless romance with the lack of pride I felt for my identity. It was so easy for him to creep into my bed. And when he withheld touch, I was more eager to be held. He treated me with such derision. Why did I need him? How many other women had there been? I knew only of Nora. She was my savior. Poor Nora.

Oh, Nora, Nora, Nora, what have you done? I thought. *What have you done?* Like all beautiful things, he would find a way to transform her into a withdrawn and tethered mute. He would degrade her, just as he degraded everyone.

I punched my mattress. *I have to stop thinking about this.* I reached for the stack of magazines and unopened mail that my mother had placed on top of my bedside table. Among the pile were a few photography magazines, a credit card offer, the latest copy of *The Wall Street Journal,* and a brochure from an art gallery that read *Eighteenth-Century Nudes.*

I flipped open the brochure and scrutinized the curves of the nude women. They were such pretty little things, I thought again. Then, there it was, icing on the mud pie—an envelope from my father stuck between the pages. Jack handled most of his letters by courier and they usually came as a surprise, this moment included. He often wrote vague notes about my childhood. The ducks, the geese, our time spent by the pool, lab experiments with my dolls, the microbes in the cave—distant memories that only widened the time-lapse between us. So much had changed. Yes, I was grateful for the bank checks that accompanied his nostalgic letters, but more than that, they gave me the feeling that our relationship was artificial, that he believed he could pay for his absence, and in return, I would offer my patronage as his adoring daughter. I didn't even know where the money was coming from. I didn't know who he was anymore, but I did know the aching in Mother's eyes. Her only distraction from his duplicity was the scramble for her to make ends meet. And each check he mailed me made the guilt feel that much worse. I never knew what Mother knew and what she didn't, and had long stopped telling her, for fear of upsetting her. Yet Mother continued caring for him, the way a good friend would, and that made me angry too. I considered her ability to love him unconditionally her greatest failure, and yet I carried the same patterns into each and every one of my relationships. *Love them no matter what they do to you.* I needed to learn to put up more walls.

My head spun. Didn't he understand that this whole thing was his fault? He was the reason I did this to myself. Couldn't he leave me alone? What did he want from me now? I was tired of the act.

Exasperated, I shoved my sheets aside. The thought of my father *the martyr, the criminal,* whoever he truly claimed to be, reaching out to me with nothing to offer but a bank check and a distorted ideal of our level of familiarity—I didn't want to read his stupid letter. I didn't want anything to do with him. What I wanted—no, needed—was to reset. *Kill me now,* I thought, holding my breath.

The Moon hid behind the clouds. A feral black cat appeared at my window. "Meow," it purred, as I slammed backward against the mattress and pressed a fluffy pillow firmly into my face.

I wished for the quiet that lived within Death. I wished for stillness, for nothingness.

The cat darted away. The Moon restored itself with a magnificent blue blaze; and then it implored, "Stop. Please. You are loved. Do not forget about skies that change color and the feeling of floating in water. In Death, you will not find this."

"I'm tired," I told the Moon. "I can't continue doing this to myself."

"Please," the Moon again beseeched. "You are loved. See it in me. If not in me, see it in the sun."

"The sun. Where's the sun?"

My arms flopped to my sides. Air returned to my lungs and color to my face.

Remember, Lanna, I thought. *You deserve a pulse. Nature will take care of you. Keep your eyes open and see things as they are. Something good must come of this.*

I swept the tears from the creases of my eyes. Plucking away clumps of old mascara from my lashes, I took another deep breath and shuddered more tears.

Then I did something I did not expect would work. I held myself. Reason crept into my conscious mind. *What time is it?*

I looked at the clock. It was 3 a.m.

Ugh. There is nothing worse than 3 a.m.

My heart pounded wildly.

Nothing except 4 a.m.

All I wanted was a way to stop and start my life over.

Isn't there a way?

Perhaps there was. Perhaps I could recalibrate another way. Perhaps I could make my heart function like it once did. The way it had when I was a child.

What was I like then? What did I do?

An epiphany.

I danced.

I stood up.

What is the rhythm of a peaceful heart?

I slid a palm sideways over my breast and tapped rhythmically against my chest, swaying my hips from side to side. Tap-tap-tap, tap-tap-tap, sway and sway.

I tried again. Tap-tap-tap, tap-tap-tap. Sway and sway and sway.

You deserve a good life, I told myself, dancing.

Come on, Lanna! You can be happy! You can be loved. You can dance!

Tap-tap-tap, tap-tap-tap, sway and sway and sway and sway.

But my brain, with its potent logic, cajoled. *My dear, you of all people should know, you cannot trick your heart.*

Sure I can, I thought. If there was anyone who could, I could. Hadn't I tricked my heart into loving a sadist? Surely I could trick it to stop loving him. I could trick happiness upon myself, couldn't I?

My body tensed. The dissonance between my head and heart had led me into the whimpering caves of loneliness. The only way to stop the dissonance was to reconcile. Yes, I had fallen in love with a monster masquerading as a man, but I would not allow myself to make the same mistake again. I kissed my knees and prayed to God.

My radar for identifying love was broken. Did I believe everyone was capable of loving? I did. That was a mistake. That was *my* mistake. Was there such a man who would not take one painful moment in my life and define my entire existence by it?

I looked down at the silver envelope from my father and my stomach sank. There *was* one man.

What does Jack want?

The Moon winked. "Isn't it obvious?"

I wanted to ignore my own preliminary conclusions. *No, it can't be. He doesn't deserve my love.*

I was hardened against him. I couldn't consider it.

Ignore it, I told myself, and I picked up *The Wall Street Journal*.

CHAPTER TWELVE

"NGUYEN, WILL I SEE YOU AGAIN?"

Nguyen was half English, half Vietnamese. Her father had fled Vietnam during the war with the United States and married a wealthy Englishwoman. Two years ago, Sam's in-laws had simultaneously died of old age. He could never bring himself to call them "Mother" and "Father," as some married couples call their in-laws. When the paramedics arrived, his deceased 'rents were found hunched over an active game of poker, surrounded by empty gin bottles. At the center of the table sat both of their wedding rings and a dozen or so poker chips. The coroner presumed that the cause of death was laughter-induced cardiac arrest. Sam wanted to know what the heck was so funny. Though the loss fed into the pit of numbness that was constantly eating at him, he took solace in their passing. At least they went out together.

Swiveling his toes in the coarse beach sand, picking up sea-glass and throwing it back into the orange bucket, the memory of Nguyen spun over him like a broken washing machine. It cycled over the past, attempting to cleanse the mental images, and yet, with each new rotation, new memories surfaced. At times, the memories were an ecstasy of colorful fish swirling around inside of him. Other times, they were a reminder of how he had failed her—the only woman to show him her soul.

At first, he had not found Nguyen particularly attractive. The night they met, the bartender drugged her drink in exchange for a twenty-dollar bill from a patron. Sam unexpectedly witnessed the exchange and watched as the martini made its way over from the big-boobed bombshell of a waitress to the reserved "A" student in his *Fundamentals of Executive Leadership* course at the London School of Economics.

Frankly, he was disgusted with the idea that anyone would want to drug Nguyen, or any woman, of course. But Nguyen was not like other women. That evening, she was wearing a bulky lavender pantsuit with shoulder pads that both hid her feminine curves and accentuated the wrong ones.

That night, he took it upon himself to ensure that she made it home safely. When she meandered into the street to begin the first of many intestinal outpours of the evening, he was there to hold her hair away from her face.

When it seemed she had nothing left to hurl, he called a taxi for her. Unfortunately, he was wrong about her having nothing left to puke, and the taxi ride was a zombie movie. The driver at one point was so offended by the blatant disregard for his yellow cab's interior that he stopped to ream Sam out. The ride culminated with a slap in the face— Nguyen slapping the driver in the face, that is, and with an apology from Sam to the driver. That late night, Sam tipped the driver with whatever he found crumpled in his pockets, which wasn't much, particularly relative to his current tipping patterns.

Sam escorted Nguyen into her flat, up five flights of stairs. He fumbled through her Gucci tote for her apartment keys for nearly twenty minutes, and with her slurred permission, respectfully helped her undress. Even in her most vulnerable state, Nguyen had a self-assured temperament that he had never seen in any other woman. He removed her clothing discreetly, to all but her pink panties; set a trash bin next to her bed; and slept on the floor beside her until he was absolutely certain she was okay.

The following weekend, she unexpectedly expressed her gratitude by showing up at his flat in a jaw-dropping miniskirt and strategically disrobing him.

"The fact that you, my attractive and esteemed classmate, watched me defile myself more times than one considers humanely possible is the most embarrassing thing that has ever happened to me," she said. "I have a huge crush on you. The way you calculate those numbers. I've never seen anything like it. "

She was bold. It did not take long for Sam to recognize Nguyen's grace, despite the uncomfortable flashbacks he sometimes had of that night. Delighted with her style of fellatio, the way she used her tongue and hands somehow knowing the perfect pressure points, he clung to her longer than he ever imagined he would. Longer than he imagined he could. And now, he clung to her even more. The more he got to know her, the more the attempted assault angered him.

There was nothing wrong with her. In fact, it seemed everything was right. She was a talented woman, smart and meticulous, austere and mysterious, too. She carried herself with just the right amount of swagger. Yet, at the time, he wondered whether he could wholly love someone so distant, for she never asked questions about his childhood, and he never asked about hers. Or maybe it was that she asked and he never told her. He couldn't remember. It was one of those things that he didn't want to remember. Maybe it hurt too much. Maybe it was out of respect for one another, or out of fear, or selfishness. Or perhaps it was merely the cultural differences between them. He wasn't sure. Whatever the cause for the gulf between them, she never fully looked into his eyes, and he never fully looked into hers; at least he couldn't remember doing so.

Except once.

Why hadn't he? The thought penetrated him.

Her eyes only haunted him now. He saw them everywhere. He saw them in the ocean and in the sky. He saw them on the faces of strangers walking past him on the street. And, of course, he saw them most defiantly in their son, Vän Junior, named after his father-in-law, just as Nguyen would have chosen.

May they both rest in peace.

Vän shuffled quickly ahead of his father with his own pink pail of sea-glass and a handful of sand shovels and rakes. After several minutes of skipping ahead of his father, he stopped, dropped his pail and toys, and yelled, "Why are you so far away? Will you please play with me?"

CHAPTER THIRTEEN

JACK'S LETTERS

In the morning, a worm squirmed relentlessly under the sharp rays of the sun. Try as it may, it failed to dig itself back into the earth where the temperature was cooler. I felt sorry for it and dug the hole wider. As it quickly disappeared below the ground, I thought about Jack and the way he delivered his letters, which always drove me nuts.

Sure, Jack would send letters to the obvious places: home, the office, my college dorm room, and destinations abroad when I was on vacation. But his correspondence was also delivered to me at restaurants and bars in the wee hours of the night; on boat rides in Central Park; at hotdog stands on street corners. At my 21st birthday after-party, a beefy, half-naked nightclub bouncer with a blond Afro and a tattoo of 2Pac on one of his triceps hauled me off the dance floor and handed me a Post-it note that said "Don't forget about your mother tonight. She's probably worried as hell."

Finally, I took a deep breath, wiped my hands clean, skimmed the edges of the silver envelope from my father, and dared myself to tear it open.

The grass parted. A garden snake whizzed past. It looked as though it had somewhere very important it needed to be, or somewhere very important from which it came.

Wow, you grew up fast, I thought, as it hurried past.

In the envelope, I found a card, a document, and a check for fifteen thousand dollars that said in the memo line: "To help you get your head on straight."

Holy shit, I thought. It was the biggest check I had ever received.

The card was made of a thick vanilla stock. The enclosed document was folded into thirds. It was ordinary, except for the fact that it looked like a contract, which obviously was not ordinary, and I was too intimidated to open it without Mary. I opened the card.

MISSWIRED by Tara Makhmali

Dear Lanna,

We have arranged for an escort to meet you promptly on Friday, June 1st, at precisely 5 p.m. Go about your day as usual—he will come to you.

This is a matter of discretion. Please sign the enclosed non-disclosure agreement. We will collect it upon your arrival. The rest will be made clear in due time.

Truly yours,
—A friend of Zar

I checked the postmark; it was marked yesterday, as though he knew I'd be returning to Mother's house today, even before I knew. I couldn't comprehend how he could know such things about me, but it irked me. I flipped the card over to see if there was anything written on the other side. Nothing.

Mary appeared in a flowery bedtime nightgown that clung to her brawny bottom.

"I was wondering where you were," she said. "I didn't think you'd come back to the tree so quickly. I should have known better. Are you sick?"

"I don't know." I quivered. "May-maybe."

"Did you sleep well?"

"I did," I lied.

She smiled, knowingly. "Can I sit with you?"

"It's wet here. You know you can."

"I don't mind." She cleared a spot and sat down.

I tucked the envelope into my cardigan, hoping to avoid what I assumed would be easy practice for her upcoming interrogation.

"What's up?" She pulled the envelope out from under my sweater.

"Silver ... I see." She handed it back. "That's okay, Little Zar; I don't need to read it. I know exactly where and whom it's from."

I looked at her suspiciously. "So now you're reading my mail?"

She laughed. "Ha! You're such a smarty-pants! It doesn't take a rocket scientist to spot a letter from Dad, Lanna. It's not like you're the only one getting them."

"Fair enough," I said, inching away. "Well, I'm not in the mood to talk."

"Fine," she said. "Just don't overthink it, like you overthink everything. Use good judgment for a change, will you? It's the only way you'll ever make peace with things and stay out of trouble."

"It's not like you've made peace with things," I snapped back.

"I'm married, aren't I? How well have you done for yourself?"

Tears immediately welled up in my eyes. "How could you say that to me?"

She shrugged, and after a brief moment it was clear she knew that she had made a mistake. "I'm sorry," she said. "I didn't mean it." She leaned in, hugged me, and then asked, "So, tell me, when are you leaving? You are going to see him, are you not? You should go see him. You know you should see him, right?"

I pushed her away. "See Dad? Are you serious?" I examined her face and said, "You read my mail, didn't you?"

"You bet I'm serious, Ladybug. What does the card say?"

I looked at it. It was just like Jack to be vague. "It says after work. Next week. There'll be an escort."

"Do you know who the escort is?"

"Yeah," I replied. "Because Jack is always so forthcoming with information. You know how evasive he is with all the important details. He's either nagging me or talking about an activity we did together twenty years ago. Great, I get it: *Thanks Jack, for teaching me to tie my shoelaces. Whoopee! That must have been a real load off Mom's back!*" I rolled my eyes.

She laughed. "True, his letters don't say anything of much use, do they? But you know what, Lanna, he's still our dad. It wouldn't hurt for you to trust him a little. Even if it hurts, it'll be good for you."

I sighed and willed back tears. "I can't. Everything hurts right now. How am I supposed to trust him after what he did to all of us?"

"I know." She scooted close. "You know, my escort to Dad was pretty nice. I think you'd like him. He was pretty handsome, too. A little bulky for your taste, but he sort of reminds me of you. He's got this artsy vibe to him, but you wouldn't recognize it straightaway."

I was taken aback. "What? You're telling me you went to see Jack? You kept it from me, and now there is some escort I'm supposed to care about? How could you hide something *that* important from me, Mary? I thought I could trust you. I don't want to talk to you anymore," I huffed, and stood up to leave.

"Don't go," she said, grabbing my arm. "I'm sorry. I wanted to tell you, but you weren't ready. You were abroad with that client of yours, the good one. You sounded so cheerful, and I was in a bad emotional place. You would've talked me out of it, and I would've listened to you."

I remained dismayed.

"Can you trust me for a minute? Please?" she begged. "I'm not *him*. You're not alone in this. And I was just like you. Remember that dreadful string of jerks I dated right before I met G?"

I sat down but turned away dismissively.

"Who do you think helped me figure it all out?" she asked.

"You're telling me Jack helped you?" I sneered.

"No, not exactly. I helped myself," she replied. "But if I had stopped myself from seeking clarity about what happened between him and Mom and *you know* ... *her* ... I would not have been able to understand what was going on with me."

"Let me guess. Abandonment issues. You didn't think you were worthy, or some bullshit like that."

"No, Lanna, it's not that simple. It's never what anyone thinks. The textbook labels are what people think they know. They're not error-proof. They're always evolving. And, usually, people don't know what they think they know. That's why I make so much money litigating. Because of how stupid smart people actually are. Think about this for a minute. When you're a kid, you are taught to listen and to believe most of what you hear from older people. But what do they actually know about you? What are those "abandonment issues," really? Do they even apply? You and I stagnated over one incident because everyone thought they were being helpful, when in fact they were giving us a cesspool of generic advice meant to solve the types of problems that we didn't have. Isn't that silly? And you can't blame those folks, either. They were just looking out for us."

"So?"

"So, you're in advertising. You make labels for a living. Society believes a lot of fluff, doesn't it? And you, my dear sister, cannot be lazy and self-hating about your own life. Compared to the masses, you're amazing, and you have to look past all of those labels and figure out what's true for you. Not in a stubborn, holier-than-thou way. In a thoughtful way."

"Now I'm lazy? Thanks."

"Are you serious? That's what you took away from what I was saying?"

"Not exactly."

She sighed. "Okay, can you please stop worrying about how you want people to see you and start worrying about what you want to see in yourself? Conferring with Dad helped me figure out my truth. All I am saying is that maybe it will help you answer some tough questions about who you are, who you want to be, and what *you* want."

"But I feel as though every time I think I have life figured out, and I start asking myself those questions, I do something that makes me sick to my stomach. I don't understand myself, Mary. Why did I let myself fall in love with that man?"

She leaned over and hugged me tight. "Were you really in love with him?"

"I don't know," I said. "I think so."

"It wasn't your fault." She held me and rocked me back and forth. "You cannot be ashamed of yourself for falling in love. But maybe you have to learn to put some walls up in new places and let some down in others. Just a thought. I swear, sis, if you let yourself learn from this, you will be all right. Better than all right. And I'm going to make sure that loser gets what's coming to him."

I began crying. "Don't bother," I said. I lay my head on her shoulder. "I'm so tired of this. It's too exhausting. I just want to forget it ever happened."

She held me tight. "And you will. Trust me. You always do better in the summertime. We both do, and I can already see the apples come in on the trees. It's going to be a broiling one."

It was true. The winter always depressed me, the spring melted my depression away slowly, and by summer, I was always beaming.

Mary sat with me until I stopped sobbing and then she left to find our mother. I stayed behind to take solace in the trees. I began daydreaming, digressing into the narrows of my subconscious, when two blue jays (one tall, the other small) appeared out of the limbs of the oak and landed right beside me on the rock where I was sitting. It gave me the chills. I sipped my bitter coffee and waited to see what they would do next. The little one plopped himself into my hair. I chuckled. He probably thought it was a nest. The other shook his leg and zigzagged until it reached a low-hanging branch. As I inspected him peck at his feathers, it became clear that his wing was broken, that he was injured. A moment later, the blue jay in my hair capered up to his companion's branch.

Upon experiencing this, a new thought, a feeling emerged: I was destined to help someone. And then another sensation blossomed: I dearly missed that someone, whoever he or she was. A vision came to me. In it, I saw a man with hollow eyes and a stodgy blue tie. His eyes, which could once see, had been plastered shut with heavy cement, and he had a little boy beside him—his son. The boy had lost something. Someone. I wondered, how did I know them? Had I seen them on television? Perhaps we were tied together in some faint way. No. More likely, I was, as always, just making things up, searching for a way to connect with whatever I felt was missing from inside me.

A golden buck galloped past. Soon, the same deer would dispose of its long, gorgeous antlers. I would find them in the woods and add them to the collection of knick-knacks I kept hidden beneath my bed.

After a week of wallowing in self-pity, while Mother did her best to cheer me up by buying me as many art supplies as I wanted and forcing me to go to as many yoga classes with her as she could, I sheepishly packed my belongings ... again. The workweek ahead would be long and arduous, but, fortunately, my name was not on the four-thousand-dollar-a-month lease, which my ex had signed alone. At the time, it bothered me. "Why can't I be on the lease?" I had asked. "Because I am *the man*," he had said. Now it was a huge relief. I knew he couldn't afford the place without my paycheck, not easily.

Heidi agreed to let me stay on her pullout sofa until I could find a new place in Manhattan, and in true form, her patience and generosity humbled me. She binge-watched episodes of *Sex and the City* with me while I sobbed on her couch, contemplating my romantic problems and comparing each male protagonist, none of whom actually seemed quite as sinister, to my ex.

Three days after sleeping on Heidi's couch and a pathetic red-eyed shuffle to and from work, Heidi began encouraging me to start looking for my own apartment. "It's what you've always wanted," she reminded me, and I took the hint. Lethargically, I called my real estate agent, Barb—she had found me my last few places—and told her I was in the market again.

"Are you sure you want *my* help?" Barb asked, as if there was something wrong with me for asking.

"Sure, why wouldn't I?" I responded. "You've been my agent for years."

She hesitated. "I guess you're right. You're not dating anyone new, are you?"

"No," I replied. "That's not a nice thing to say. Why are you acting so judgmental all of a sudden? You've never cared about my love life before."

"Oh, no. I didn't mean to make you feel that way," she replied. "I thought maybe *I* was the bad luck."

"I doubt that," I replied, thinking that it was a weird thing for her to say.

The next day, as the two of us inspected a promising studio apartment on a tree-lined street in an up-and-coming neighborhood on the Upper, Upper East Side of Manhattan, Barb broke out in a sweat and confessed.

"I slept with your ex," she said, quivering. "He choked me in the middle of coitus. Afterward, he told me he wouldn't pay my fee, unless I wanted him to tell my boss that I was *shtupping* my clients. I'm sorry. You can keep my fee, if you want," she offered me as a consolation.

My stomach did somersaults. "It's okay," I told her. "Look at the upside. At least he didn't photograph you while plowing you and then upload the nudes onto the Craigslist ad he was using to relist his apartment."

"He did that to you?" she replied.

"Yep," I said. "But my sister got the cops to force him to take it down. And you want to know what else?" I asked her, half grinning, half ready to vomit. "The tagline on his LinkedIn profile page now says *F*cker Who Abuses Women and Takes Long Bowel Movements on the Company Dime*. He's going to lose his mind when he sees it."

Her eyes widened with fear or empowerment, I couldn't tell.

"You *did not* do that. Did you?"

"I did," I said, forcing out a laugh. "All he cares about is what employers think of him. It's the best trick I could come up with. His connections are dropping like flies."

"Aren't you afraid he'll retaliate?"

"No," I said. "Well, a little. But if he does, I'll tell him it wasn't me; that it must have been one of the other women he's been with. He's obviously done terrible things to a lot of women, and I bet they'd all be happy to see him suffer. There's a reason his contacts are vanishing without questioning him." I caught a whiff of something. "By the way, it smells terrible in here. Like rotting cabbage and dirty underwear. Wait a minute, what are those? Are those *pubes* on the kitchen counter?"

We both stepped forward to take a closer look.

I jumped back. "Yep. And that, right there," I gulped, "is a mouse."

The mouse paused, looked up, startled, and then fiercely scampered across the parquet floor, under the bed in the living room, and into a hole in the wall near the radiator.

"No way. I'm not living here. You're going to have to work a little harder for that fee," I said.

"Uh-huh," she replied. "Are you sure? If you hire a cleaning service, this would be a charming apartment. It's a steal for the square footage."

I thought about it for a moment. The price was right. "Sure. I guess so. It is a good deal." I ate my pride. "Okay, I'll take it." But after another whiff that ended with me awkwardly dry-heaving into my own hands, I determined, "This place sucks. I'm not taking it. It doesn't need a cleaning, it needs an exorcism."

Barb laughed as she followed behind. "You're right. It's not worth it." And then she paused. "What if I could get the landlord to lower the price even more?"

I rolled my eyes. *Realtors.*

PART THREE

PART THREE

CHAPTER FOURTEEN

A STORM IN A TEACUP

The day of reckoning had arrived. An escort, whoever and wherever he was from, was supposed to come falling out of the sky "at precisely 5 p.m." to whisk me away from my beloved entourage of creative soldiers and bring me off to a place that I didn't want to go. To. See. My. Father.

I could feel a queasy, uneasy sensation growing in the left side of my gut, the way I always had as a child when I thought of Father's life in prison. Though I never wanted to see him again, I couldn't bear the thought of him in jail. I couldn't bear the thought of him chained and beaten as though he were a—I couldn't bring myself to say the word "slave." Even the word gave me a pang of pain, as the violence of the mind's imaginations ran fearfully through my brain.

He was my father. He didn't belong there. I was so angry with him.

As an adult, I shunned it all. Even the seediest of men, I thought, had within them the opportunity to change, not that *I* wanted to change them, but simply that I could see hope within them—a sort of hope that everyone discarded as misbelief, as lies, as a mirage.

I had made no attempt to see him in jail. My stomach couldn't handle it. What had they done to him in there? I didn't want to know. As a child, my grandparents made up mollifying stories to force back their home-cooking whenever the topic arose. "It's not a normal prison, dear," they'd say. "He lives in the prison of his heart." I had no idea what that meant. "Then why would he choose to live in a real one?" I'd demand. Their calm, quiet looks never satisfied me. What were they hiding from me?

***

At 4:30 p.m., I surveyed the perimeter of my company's glittering open-office space and tried to figure out whether I could leisurely exit or whether I would be called into another meeting and would need to duck out before getting caught leaving. My office mate was in the bathroom, preparing for a date. She returned reeking of marijuana and perfume. "Can I get some of that?" I asked, and she handed me a bottle of Versace perfume, as though she didn't know what I was suggesting, but after I smiled and winked, she grinned, slipped her one-hitter up my sleeve, and warned, "It's strong. Go easy on it."

I dropped the piece into my purse, a Chloe tote that I had purchased from a vintage designer clothing store for five hundred bucks cash, and made my way toward the ladies' room. A few stray executives wandered past, no one involved enough to know schedules—not the real schedules, that is. If you work in industry, you know there are always two: the one for the executives and the one for people living in reality. The rest were friends. They'd cover for me. I hadn't burned all my bridges during last week's soap opera episode of *Days of Lanna's Pathetic Life*.

When I arrived at the stalls, I pulled the ominous card from Jack, along with the signed contract, out of my tote. I took a hit of the weed, blew the smoke up into the vent, and tried not to cough. The invite didn't provide me with any indication of who the escort was, where the escort would meet me, or where Jack and I would eventually meet. I assumed, as Mary had alluded to, that the escort would be one of Jack's friends from our hometown university, a relative of some sort—*why else would Mary say he reminded her of me?*

If there was a silver lining to my stomach pangs, it was that my slender stomach sat just right between my wide hips and self-supporting C-cup breasts, and this sometimes gave me a slight competitive advantage when I had the desire to actually pursue a man; at least I told myself it did, as I took another hit and wondered about the man taking me to prison. I left the stall, searched my tote for eye drops, and instead found mascara, which I layered on, and a peppermint, which I popped under my tongue.

When I returned, Boss's door was wide open. This was bad news. Correction. Terrible news. It meant I was expected to pull another stupid all-nighter, which, given how little I was sleeping these days, wouldn't have made much of a difference to my physical state, but I was committed to being wherever my father was committed, as much as that scared me.

There was a signal Boss sent the team with the opening and closing of her door. She was probably unaware that we all knew how to read the signal.

At any point after 4 p.m., when the door was open, it meant that Hangry Boss (also known as pissed-off-from-hunger reckless Boss) was ready to take charge of something that didn't need taking charge of. Whoever was near and whatever useless project was furthest from people's minds was suddenly at risk. She'd begin by spewing insults and insistences disguised as compliments. "Janette," she'd call out to her divorced assistant in the hallway, and from behind her oversized executive desk, "Nice work reorganizing my calendar! Too bad you couldn't do the same for your pathetic marriage!" She'd chuckle. "Now where's that list?"

The list was a hodgepodge of irrational and fictitious work that was never assigned, and yet the items were overdue on the spot. She did this while sporting a cunning smile. Whenever you thought she might be dishing out a slice of something delicious, soon you'd realize that the mozzarella had fully soured, but you had already eaten the whole damn pie.

Her compliments were rotten, unlocked and definitely loaded, which triggered a whirlwind of unnecessary *URGENT* overnight tasks that made my heart panic just thinking about it.

We all obliged for fear of retaliation, or sometimes, sheer absentmindedness, and come morning, she'd publicly congratulate herself. "Without my leadership skills," she would say, "we'd all be a bunch of losers."

And I'd agree with her, because part of it was true; I was a loser. Why was I still working there?

Heidi called it a "storm in a teacup."

"That's a cute way to put it," I told her. "It's more like a loaf in a running john, and I'm the janitor."

This completely grossed her out, and at the same time, gave me a new respect for hotel maids.

In the end, my team grew close because of it, so I suppose that was positive.

C'mon, C'mon, C'mon. Please shut, I pleaded with Boss's frosted glass door.

After a few minutes, Boss rose from her seat, walked to the door, and spotted my glance.

I ducked behind my computer.

She smiled and clicked the door shut, only to crack it open again seconds later. The speakerphone dial tone on her conference phone beeped. I heard numbers as they were entered. A silver spoon clanked against the edges of a ceramic mug.

"I've told you this twice now. I want it now. ASAP! Do you know what *now* means? Get it to me now! I'm scheduling an urgent meeting. I want you, Frank" (presumably someone's supervisor), "and the entire creative team ready. You're going to do what I tell you to do. I swear, I have the B-team on this project, bunch of losers."

I grabbed my tote and packed my belongings as quickly as I could. I pushed aside several books I was reading all at once (I never could just stick to one) and rushed to grab my raincoat. If I did not leave the office now, I'd have to come up with a solid excuse for why I couldn't stay, and I couldn't think of a Single. Damn. Thing.

I plotted. *Okay, what can I do to make it look like I'm here?*

Carefully, I placed my pashmina over the back of my chair, and then I pushed my chair slightly away from my desk.

My thoughts raced. *What else? What else?*

I took a deep breath and turned my green desk lamp from OFF to ON. The light shone perfectly onto a redlined graphic I was tinkering with.

God, I hope this works.

Hopefully, it would. Hopefully, it would look as though I was in the bathroom, at a meeting, or in the break room, and that I would return, when, in reality, I had escaped to the weekend, where I would, without hesitation, turn my BlackBerry (I still couldn't believe that's what they made us use) off and leave it uncharged at the bottom of a bottomless purse.

I hurried to the side-elevator entrance, where I pressed the down-arrow button as hard and as repeatedly as my index finger could handle. I pressed so hard that my finger clicked.

Boss's voice echoed in the hall.

I panicked. The idea of being caught, together with the surreal adrenaline of being high, plunged my thoughts into paranoia. *Oh, why does this building have to have so many floors? What's so great about skyscrapers? Aren't shorter buildings less costly to maintain? What's the deal with tourists snapping photographs of* the fountain out front? It's not a great fountain. Go to Europe if you want fountains! Stupid tourists!

CHAPTER FIFTEEN

CONTRACTIONS

Nguyen slammed her cell phone onto the table. The contractions were growing closer together. She looked down at her belly. "Dammit, where is he?"

She couldn't remember the last time she could see her nether-bits. Early in her pregnancy, she cared about what might happen as her belly grew. Now it had grown from a perfect landing strip into a wild and unkempt jungle, and she didn't give a shit.

The sky was gray and black. The local newscasters had fussed over the severity of the storm, but she had not believed them. Nor had Sam. His only concern had been whether to head to work earlier that morning, and indeed, he did. He left two hours earlier, 4 a.m., to ensure that he would arrive to work on schedule. A hypothetical storm wasn't going to puncture his always-punctual and never-late track record, not if he could control it.

The plan was for Nguyen to deliver the baby with a midwife—no nurses, no doctors, no drip, and no unnecessary knife branding her glorious, bountiful body.

Her father, Vän, had convinced her mother, Victoria, to do the same in the summer of 1976, the year Nguyen was born. The dialogue went something like this:

***

"Let's hire a doula," her father had said to her mother. "We'll all be better for it."

Her mother had protested. "Only pagans and poor people have babies outside the hospital."

But after meeting with the lovely doula her father had convinced her to interview, her mother agreed it was "appropriate," and that a doctor's presence would be more meddlesome than helpful during her healthy and routine pregnancy, and the doula whom Vän—Nguyen's father—had identified was such a delight that the mere idea of her presence solidified the sentiment that her mother could (and would) have her baby at a nursing center rather than in a hospital.

At first, her mother had decided she did not want her husband present in the labor room, which, for a woman of her mother's status and the generation in which the delivery was to occur was the prescribed "right thing to do." But mid-labor, her mother, to put it mildly, "requested" Vän's presence, and Vän, of course, knowing there was no deeper cruelty than to abandon a laboring woman in her hour of need, secured his wife's legs up over her head, and called out to her with confident encouragement until Nguyen's buttery body came sliding out into the doula's hands.

***

It was a story that Nguyen's parents often shared. She cherished it.

A contraction took hold of Nguyen's body. She held on to it as if it were an ocean wave, bellowing as she reached the tip and trailing off as it dissolved.

Something felt off. A hot, sharp sensation scraping inside of her like an alley cat scratching against the glass of a window, only the window was her flesh; the cat was her child.

She picked up her phone and redialed Sam.

It rang twice and went straight to voicemail. Midway through leaving a message, she lost service.

She flipped on the television to Channel 7 News:

"Due to 70-mile-an-hour gusts, cell towers servicing the northern region of Hunterdon County have been damaged.

Tornado warnings remain in effect. At this time, we urge you to seek safety ..."

Frantically, she grabbed her car keys. Everything about her pregnancy had been perfect.

Everything but this.

When the contractions first hit, she thought it was a false alarm. *Braxton Hicks*, she concluded. *No big deal. I can handle this.*

Then they increased in severity. The sharpness increased. At 35 weeks, *this was not part of the plan.*

She opened the sliding door to the driveway. Another painful contraction erupted. She leaned against the doorway for support, trying hard not to clench her body.

Don't make it worse than it needs to be, she told herself, remembering what she had learned in class.

She stepped out. The wind shot her long, silky black hair off her back and into the sky like a torpedo. Perspiration covered her forehead.

The apple tree in the front yard blossomed. In a burst of euphoria, Nguyen smiled. She walked swiftly down the driveway. The baby kicked. She held her belly.

"You're going to be okay, little one," she said aloud, hoisting her enormous body upward into the truck.

I can do this. I can do this. I can do this.

Sam always teased her for purchasing the truck. Of all the vehicles she could have chosen, she chose a blue Ford pickup. He felt it didn't belong in their driveway.

"It's not very *you*," he had said to her, alluding to the contrast between her flair for couture and its—

How had he put it? She tried to remember. *Oh, yes,* she giggled to herself. The bumper was scratched and nearly falling off. "*Hillbilly-ness.*"

It was an older model. It looked out of place in front of their elaborate stucco home.

"You're wearing a three thousand dollar belt and that truck cost you, what? A thousand bucks?" he had said.

She didn't care. There was something special about it. She loved it. There was a feeling about it. It made her feel more—

What was it, specifically?

Ah, yes, that was it. "American."

For her, the United States, by and large, was a racist place to live, far more racist than where she grew up in the U.K. Despite marrying Sam, it took tremendous time and effort for her to earn her U.S. citizenship.

When the government finally granted her citizenship, she knew she would still need to work hard to overcome the ridicule that her Vietnamese complexion engendered. Like everyone else, she wanted to blend in. And, like any woman, she wanted, simply, to feel safe.

In her mind, there was nothing more American than the blue Ford pickup. Symbolically, it represented the affinity she felt toward the U.S. for embodying the values of freedom and happiness—values she held dear, despite her father's feelings about the U.S. during the Vietnam War.

She held the Declaration of Independence as close to her heart as she sometimes held Sam, occasionally reciting the words aloud early in their courtship, when he didn't have much money, though she was born into money, and the going had gotten tough for him:

"We hold these truths to be self-evident, that all men are created equal; that they are endowed by their Creator with certain unalienable rights; that among these are life, liberty, and the pursuit of happiness."

"The pursuit of happiness," he would say. "That's the lie we tell the poor to keep them poor."

Of course, pragmatically, the truck was a sturdy, well-made piece of machinery. She would fix the bumper, and she was proud to pay for it in cash.

Also, and perhaps more importantly, it was a finger to anyone who told her she was not American, which she enjoyed dangling whenever she was feeling particularly bloated.

The baffled looks of other drivers, expecting to see a straw-eating, butt-crack-showing, tattooed American hillbilly, only to find a pregnant Vietnamese businesswoman grinning at them and giving them the middle finger, was, well, devilishly satisfying.

Of course, it never diminished the skepticism of the white-and-wealthy. They harbored a breed of subtle, *educated* racism. To them, the truck only highlighted her otherness.

She climbed behind the wheel. Sitting within its thick metal walls, she felt tall, sturdy, and strong. The engine purred. The rain thudded softly against the windshield.

She turned down the road and onto the on-ramp to the highway. The contractions eased. There was a moment of rest.

Phew, she thought. *Forty-five minutes is all I need to get to the closest hospital. I can handle this.*

Another contraction took hold. She clenched. The roads were slippery. Thunder beat like a tribal drum between contractions.

She startled and jerked. The resting period ended more quickly than anticipated. Her contractions had grown irregular. She could no longer relax between them. There was no rhythm to them, and no mechanism to time them. They came abruptly and unexpectedly.

Vomit flowed up from her intestines and then went back down. Tears stung her cheeks. She bit her lip, gripped the wheel, and channeled the pain into her mighty blue Ford.

Then lightning struck. Followed by thunder. Followed by lightning again. Sparks of electricity whipped fiercely at the road ahead. She swerved, frantically exiting off the highway onto a narrow dirt road.

She had no idea where she was. She didn't want to stop. She couldn't stop. She had to keep moving. The fog was coming. The baby was coming. Soon she would be lost in heat. Lost in blackness.

Another contraction took over. Its wave seared her body. The pressure between her legs sharpened. Blood poured out from between them.

She slammed the breaks. Her wheels spun out of control. Skidding off the road, lightning struck the truck. She blacked out.

CHAPTER SIXTEEN

THE ELEVATOR INCIDENT

Thank God. The elevator had arrived. I darted inside.

Grimy blankets hung from the elevator walls. Wood shavings dusted the floor. I slammed the CLOSE DOOR button several times, anxiously waiting for the doors to glide shut. Two men standing side by side in the elevator halted their conversation to watch my frantic button-slamming frenzy.

I blushed, and stared down at my pointy stilettos. Slicing them against the steel elevator floors in the interminable wait for the doors to close, I tried not to grind my teeth, and instead, considered changing into my flip-flops.

I opted against it. I wanted to look sleek. Plus, my shoes completed my chic black-on-black with black New York City attire. *What's the hold-up? Why doesn't this darn thing close?* I pressed the button twice more.

The doors finally shut.

"Hallelujah," I muttered, and sighed a breath of relief.

Someone laughed.

I shied and looked back down at the floor, until the scent of fresh aftershave wafted into my nostrils. "Gosh, that smells delightful," I said, hesitating to address the cute strangers with my eyes since my eyes were probably a little bloodshot. I glanced up and smiled, and was immediately captivated by their combined handsomeness.

They smiled back.

On first impression, they seemed as though they were the type of men who assumed all women were flirtatious. I am not sure what gave me that impression. It could have been their posturing. Or maybe it was simply that every New York City male executive I had ever known was a smidgeon more sexist than anyone wanted to believe.

I'm over it, I told myself. *There will come a time.*

Fortunately, the fear of deliverance to my boss had dissolved, though its dissolution was premature. The service elevator ran two to three times slower than the regular elevators. Someone with large boxes and oversized machinery could rapidly trigger an express to the basement, the "man-zone," where union workers, like rowdy locker room boys, ate lunch, talked shop, and grunted. The grunting was likely a figment of my imagination. Usually, the workers were soft-spoken and polite, and, in reality, more restrained than rowdy. Nonetheless, if one of the workers were to hop on, I could conceivably end up back upstairs, where our beloved autocrat would undoubtedly revile me with one of her award-worthy temper tantrums.

Please do not let that happen. I rolled my eyes.

Of the two men in the elevator, one was older, likely in his mid-60s and probably closer to retirement. On second thought, I determined, *who am I to judge if someone is close to retirement or not?* The other man was younger. If I had to guess, I'd say he was 36. His smile alone oozed charisma.

Both men had pearly white teeth, clean shaves, and intimidatingly nice attire, even by highbrow City standards.

The older man wore an English-style tweed jacket with velvet elbow patches, a French-cuff shirt, and a pair of striking sapphire cufflinks. His burgundy leather belt matched his soft Italian leather shoes. Any layperson could see that a seamstress had meticulously arranged each stitch to complement his figure, which, in all of its mastery, could not conceal his somewhat nebulously shaped potbelly. He looked important, like he was the *Alpha*, the *Chief*.

I grinned, and for a moment I was mildly enamored with the Chief. Over the years, I had worked with many big shots with lofty résumés. But despite their affluence, they ended up being the same as everyone else, only with a little more cunning in their directives. It didn't make them any more capable at their jobs. Usually, it made them louder and more arrogant.

Chief winked. I blushed. I was too high.

The other gentleman was nicely tanned, muscular, and of a brown and probably friendly origin—European, Spanish, Italian, or possibly Turkish. He wore a modest slim-cut black tuxedo with a three-button vest over a light pink-and-white pinstripe shirt and a supple black bowtie.

The two confidants returned to their conversation:

"You're wrong, Shep. People lack self-awareness, particularly those who should know better. To uncover a person's abilities, values, and intent, you must attack without hesitation, without morality. You must offend," said Chief.

My mood darkened. I clouded into a furious fog. Chief's words reminded me of my ex. I could see him saying something violent under the guise of "don't take it personally; its just business," and suddenly I felt desperate to preserve my belief in compassion.

"Bullshit!-chu!" I mock sneezed.

Chief turned to me and grimaced. "Sweetheart," he said, his voice growing harsh. *"No one can hear you in here. Do you think you're being smart?"*

"I get it, you're the smart one," I responded, accidentally spitting into his face in what felt like slow motion.

Oh shit, I thought, gleaning his reaction. *What have I done?*

Suddenly, I was afraid. Vertigo set in as I realized, *you are a woman, alone in an elevator with two strange males.*

Chief returned his attention to the Tuxedoed Man. "Now you see, Shep. Here's a perfect learning opportunity. This young woman, Miss Zar, is it? Shouldn't she know it is unwise to ruffle the feathers of two men whom she hardly knows? And not just anywhere, but here, in an *enclosed elevator.*"

I trembled. *He knows my name?*

"She bears no control over her emotions, has no self-awareness, sneezing in that ridiculous, obvious—what would you call it?" He cackled, cocked his head sideways, and looked me up and down. "Unaware righteous delusion. Now, Shep, what's the point of being virtuous when you don't consider your safety? When you don't consider your surroundings?" Waving his finger like the stern headmaster of a rigid all-boys prep school, he continued, "Safety, safety, safety." He patronized as though I were a caged hamster on a spin-wheel. "The most basic need of being human. And look at that flushed face, *poor baby,*" he puckered. "She thinks she's being clever. How cute."

The Tuxedoed Man frowned and raised his fist.

My heart raced.

"Awww, come on now, Shep." Chief laughed and placed his hand over it. "There's no need for violence here. The idea of it is enough to get at what you want. Put your arm down. I was simply making a point. Now," he paused. "Let's make a bet. It'll be fair. I bet the next time Lanna Zar enters an elevator with two male strangers, she'll think twice about how and when she opines."

I slid myself backward into the Tuxedoed Man. He leaned me further into his chest and a buoyant wisp of my hair sprung over my forehead.

Chief stepped in closer to us. "I suppose, yes, it is true, young lady." He reached for the fallen tendril irritating my eyes and strummed it between his fingers. "If I were a kinder man, conceivably, I'd teach you *how* to think. I'd teach you to control your emotions. But, alas," he lunged rapidly, "I'm a Jack-in-the-box."

And in a millisecond, his groin was pressed firmly against my own, and I was sandwiched between the two of them. "Get off me," I demanded. "Get off!"

He faltered, rebounded quickly, and slid his cigar-like fingers into my satin blouse and lifted my laminated security badge.

"LANNA ZAR, Creative Ad," he spoke loudly, holding the ID steadily up to my face to ensure I would feel his wrath.

And just like that, I remembered my place in the world. Lanna Zar. Daughter of convicted criminal. Abused ex-girlfriend. Loser. Lost soul. Here for your erotic taking.

I shuddered to my own name, which hung from my neck like a noose.

"So adorable," Chief concluded, seemingly delighted by my sulking face. "But alas," he sighed, "I am a married man and I don't have the energy to spar with little twats and their make-believe superheroes." He slapped the badge hard against my abs, and smiled elegantly at the Tuxedoed Man as though he was due for a little gratitude. "Now, that, Shep, is how you offend with the intent to teach. Will she learn? Only time will tell."

The elevator stopped. The Tuxedoed Man appeared furious. The doors opened. Tourists gathered to take photographs. Security officers loitered. Chief exited the elevator. My heart skipped a beat.

F'ing New York, I thought, forcing back tears. I felt dizzy, then nauseated, and a moment later I was swinging sideways from the elevator blankets like a lowland gorilla trying to get my bearings.

Shoo, I thought, of the Tuxedoed Man, who was still in the elevator watching me make a fool of myself. *Go away. I don't want your help. Leave me alone.*

I didn't want to be seen this way. Or maybe seen ever again.

I had to be stealthy, didn't I? I scolded myself. *I couldn't ride the main elevator, could I? I had to get stoned and pick a fight with an old coot.*

I was deeply embarrassed, and at the same time, very thirsty.

CHAPTER SEVENTEEN

THE SHAWL

When Nguyen regained consciousness, her truck was wrapped around a boulder, her door had been crushed inward, and she was encircled by shattered plastic. She wiggled her limbs. They throbbed. Blood covered her hands. Her slender legs were caught in metal. She was trapped. She strained to release herself from it. She bit down on her seat belt and pulled her legs up with her hands, but it didn't work—the metal lodged further into her body. She howled. And then she remembered. *The baby.* She gasped and clutched her belly. He had stopped wiggling, but for how long? *Was he dead?*

She bellowed again, this time plunging her torso as far forward as her body would allow, and clenching her quads. Still nothing. She tried again. Nothing. Again. Nothing. Each time, the metal lodged deeper, the pain scaling up and down her skeleton as it peeled her skin straight from her bones.

The rain banged on, and with it, time and whimpers fatigued. The dimming prospect that no one would ever come to her rescue grew more and more likely. How long had she been stranded there? How much more pain would she be able to endure?

She fell into a helpless dance of spasms that stirred when lightning struck and that quieted when vicious downpours flooded into the truck.

Thunder grew closer. A massive bolt struck. She shrunk in desperation. *Why are you doing this to me, God?* she questioned, the thought floating up from her mind like a wayward balloon.

Then she felt something in her stomach shift. A kick. Her baby, he kicked. Her eyes widened. She swallowed her fear, her agony, and as she relaxed her eyelids, she felt his light shining inside her, and with him, the call of duty jolted her back into action.

"Help me," she howled, harvesting another kick, another contraction, and another spate of lightning flurries into the loudest call for help she could muster.

Thirty seconds passed. Another contraction came. Another went. *I'm going to die,* she thought, squinting into the fog through an opening in the heap. And then, as though the balloon of thoughts she had released earlier into the sky had heard her prayer, there it was—a cape, a lavender shawl, flapping wildly in the wind. The wearer of the shawl, a middle-aged woman, was running toward her.

"Are you all right?" the woman yelled, her question absconded by the blowing wind.

Nguyen howled. Another contraction took hold. "He's coming. My baby is coming. You have to save him. Are you real?"

The woman quickly confirmed. "I'm real!"

"There's a hammer somewhere. My legs are stuck. Call for help."

The woman spun in and out of every crevice she could access, searching for the hammer. The rain pounded.

Nguyen panicked. "Please, lady. My baby. You've got to get me out of here."

CHAPTER EIGHTEEN

THE SHEEP & SHEPPARD

The Tuxedoed Man, Luke Sheppard ("Shep") stood quietly in the elevator. It seemed he too was embarrassed. It seemed as though he wanted to console me. "Ms. Zar, are you okay?" he asked politely, extending his palm over the small of my back and analyzing my eyes for the answer.

I held his hand to regain my posture and nudged him away. "I'm fine. Thank you."

"Are you sure? Fine, like a parking ticket?" he said, attempting to lighten the mood.

"What?" I responded, frazzled. "Oh, haha, funny, yes, thank you. I could use some space."

He nodded, and exited into the marbled lobby where my assailant was waiting.

What a piece of work, I thought, watching him scamper off. *I should say something.*

A security officer poked his head around the corner. "You all right?" he asked. "The elevator stuck?"

I shook off the high (and the low) and plowed through the door. "Yeah, fine," I said, still distraught. "Like a parking ticket."

He scratched his head. "Okay, you have a good weekend now. I'll have Maintenance take a look."

"Sure," I said. "You, too." I paused. "You ever see those two guys before?"

"Uhhh, which ones?"

"The rich old man with the awkwardly shaped potbelly and the guy in the tux. The guys who just came through here."

"Oh, Old Chuck? Yeah, I've seen him before. He always takes the back door. Tips well. Why? He give you a hard time? He comes off mean, curse'n 'bout women and employees and all that, but he's *real* nice. One time he heard me arguing with my supervisor about sick-leave pay and he sunk a wad of bills into my sleeve like that." He flicked his wrist and snapped loudly. "If I didn't get that green, boy oh boy, my boy wouldn't-a had no winter coat that winter. For a dirty-mouthed old man, he's a real class act." He grinned. "Why? He do something nice for you too?"

I wanted to puke. *I wish.* For a second I thought about telling him what had happened in the elevator. But it was pointless.

"Something like that," I said. "What about the other guy? The one in the tux, with the thick eyebrows and the pink shirt. Have you seen him before?"

"Let me think." He scratched his head. "Nope. Never. He work for Old Chuck?"

"Don't know," I said. "Forget I mentioned it." I made a beeline through the revolving doors onto the busy sidewalk.

Whatever pathetic self-worth I had, two complete strangers did not have the right to do what they did in that elevator. Not without my say-so.

I spotted them from a short distance. My heart raced. Tuxedoed Man was angry; he was scowling and shaking his head at Chief, who, in return, was squealing nonchalantly. I pumped myself up to approach them. *You don't scare me, you mean old potbellied pig,* I told myself. *Do you know who I am? I'm Lanna Zar. You don't mess with the daughter of a criminal. I'm com'n for you.* I looked down at my name badge again.

"LANNA ZAR."

My heart stopped. *This is stupid.* All I ever wanted was to be known for something other than being the criminal daughter of Jack Zar. I dropped my badge again. I wasn't fighting anyone.

***

"I don't know. This isn't you," Shep said.

Chuck cackled. "Oh, c'mon now, Shep, she's a smart girl. No one's hurt."

"You are a disturbed man." He quickly turned away. "You're going to pay for this."

The old slimebag shooed him off and listlessly plodded to the bar around the corner, where you could see him through the window skirting past the host. "Scotch, please," he was probably saying to the bartender.

***

Shep wanted to tell Lanna *you're safe.* He wanted to tell her it was purely bad timing that the annual investors' bowtie lunch had been scheduled for the same day on which he had agreed to escort her to the Oates Estate, and that it was *his* mistake for believing he could ever casually disclose his personal agenda to a rich old clown.

Had it been any other day, he would not have engaged in this forced hobnobbing. This is not how he had imagined this moment would play out. The more Shep pondered this, the more upset he grew with himself. How would he explain this to Jack?

One good deed each month. That's all he aspired to do. And the opportunities did not present themselves the way one would anticipate, not the worthwhile ones anyway. Jack had shyly asked for his help. That couldn't have been easy for Jack.

What bothered Shep most was not his own imperfect elevator intervention, but that there was a morsel of truth to the old loon's warning. Lanna had been alone in an enclosed elevator with two men she didn't know. She had been protesting and spitting. He hadn't expected her to be so loose-lipped. That wasn't how Jack had described her. And, he hadn't expected her to be so mysteriously beautiful either.

Some escort I am. He shook his head and looked down at his watch. 5:10 p.m. "I'm late," he said, turning the corner. Waving, he hoped to grab Ms. Zar's attention. She, of course, was observing his every move. A burst of warm air blew her long curly hair away from her bright, spotless face. Her eyes were blackened from smudged mascara. Her skin glistened. She pursed her glossy lips, forming the semblance of a smile. Even in distress, there was something about her.

His heart stopped—she was gorgeous. He was struck by an energy, a pull between them. *Without words, everyone is gorgeous.* He wondered if she was aware of the strange sort of magnetism he was feeling. As any gentleman would, he bent his arm into a triangle and hoped she would slip her arm through. He second-guessed himself. *Why would she cling?*

PART FOUR

CHAPTER NINETEEN

SLIP THROUGH MY FINGERS

I fell into a deep silence and followed alongside Shep. For no explicable reason, I felt comforted by his presence, and yet the more I thought, the less I could make sense of the encounter in the elevator. The old pervert had thrown a monkey wrench into my instincts.

Shep was clearly aroused. He scanned over my eyes and my curves. He obviously had lost himself in my shapes. His pupils dilated. He glided beside me, blushing as he elbowed the swarms of oblivious pedestrians as though to protect us both.

We walked past the hole-in-the-wall bodega with the blinking "Lottery Tickets Here" sign, where I often popped in to grab a blood orange-flavored San Pellegrino, a six-piece container of premade sushi, a quarter pound of fresh burrata cheese, and a small homemade chicken empanada. The Chinese woman who ran the store, and Juan, the hefty black-haired Mexican chef who ran the deli, never thought twice about my odd assortment of selections. Of all the City had to offer—the blazing lights of Broadway, the grandeur of erudite museums, shopping on Fifth Avenue, the comfort of diners, the sex appeal of restaurants and bars on every block, the perpetual smell of coffee, pizza, pastries, hot dogs, and falafels—the one thing I appreciated most about living in the City was the fact that I could often order Polly-O string cheese, dumplings, and chocolate mousse cake all from the same establishment. There was nowhere else quite like New York.

After several blocks, Shep started chuckling to himself.

Boy, this guy is weird, I thought.

He halted and finally managed to shake the goofy smile from his face. "We are way off track. Jack sent me. I'm a friend. We're heading in the wrong direction."

"No shit." I smiled confidently at him. "Who the heck was the other guy in the elevator? I hope he is not one of Jack's friends too."

"No, he's not a friend; he's more like a wealthy acquaintance." He sounded sheepish. "I don't know what his problem is. He's an ass. I can make up excuses for him, but I won't. All I can tell you is that sometimes when people are sick, their minds turn sick first. He's a rich drunk with a broken heart—the worst kind of sick. His wife recently had an affair."

"And the bastard is taking it out on all women? Nice guy. Real nice. Some company you keep."

He reddened. "I'm sorry. I was careless. I mentioned that you were my good deed for the month."

I glowered at him.

"That didn't come out right either," he sighed, and placed a hand to his forehead. "I'm here to help facilitate a meeting between you and Jack—your father. Nothing else. We're a ways away, and it's going to be a long trip. I am sorry we started it this way. Please, can you follow me?"

"My mother told me never to talk to strangers," I sassed, feeling apprehensive yet still curious about the whole thing. "But it's okay. I don't have much to lose, and I don't expect my meeting with Jack to be pleasant. Are you the one who sent the card?"

"Not quite," he replied. "But you'll meet her."

Her, I thought. *Finally, the possibility of sanity.*

CHAPTER TWENTY

FOLLOW THE MASS

An hour on the subway, followed by another five by rail, and the journey to Jack began to feel endless. Shep and I spent hours quietly smiling at one another, enjoying the intimacy of our silence.

I was growing ready to unravel Shep's bowtie, unbutton his shirt, and slip myself between his legs.

But I knew better. He was not the right fit for me. I could hear Mother's voice buzzing in the back of my head, trying to teach me a thing or two about timing and judgment. *"When he flirts with you, turn away; you don't want him to think you're 'that' kind of girl."* Of course, she was usually right, but unfortunately, I sometimes was *"that" kind of girl*.

Looking at his broad-built shoulders, his muscular chest, and slender, solid waist, I determined that whatever attraction I harbored for him was not related to his physique. If anything, his mass disappointed me. *Follow the mass and you will find a stupid man,* I thought.

The smoothness of his skin, on the other hand—I drifted back into my fantasy.

Shep was counting the wisdom lines on his palms. He suddenly noticed my gaze and his cheeks reddened. He loosened his bowtie and unbuttoned the top buttons of his shirt, revealing his caramel-colored flesh.

"Is it hot in here?" he asked.

"A little," I said, pouting. "What's the occasion?"

The teenage girl in the next aisle of seats started playing the radio app on her phone while using her camera to apply her rouge.

"You look vulnerable without your bowtie," I said, smirking at the teenager.

"Vulnerable?" He smiled and shrugged.

I uncrossed my legs and slid off my heels. My toenails were a silvery blue that I had painted in layers to resemble the night sky. Leaning back into the leathery seat, I pretended to accidentally caress his leg with my own.

"Vulnerable like a virgin," I said. "Touched for the very first time."

The teenage girl laughed and chimed in. "Madonna is so old. But she's still a classic."

Shep laughed bashfully and adjusted himself.

I enjoyed flirting, though I could see that Shep was growing uneasy. I smiled remorselessly. "I'm sorry. We can be friends. Can I be your friend?"

His eyes glimmered. I got lost in them.

He cleared his throat. "My truck is parked at the station. When we arrive, I will drop you off out in front. I'm doing this as a favor to Jack," he said authoritatively, as though he were reminding himself.

"Oh, right," I replied, suddenly taken aback by the overwhelming thought of facing Jack, coupled with the ugly feeling of being rejected. I let my hair fall over my eyes, turned away, and began rummaging through my handbag for my iPhone, which was no doubt buried somewhere at the bottom of my purse, probably next to a tampon and a wad of chewed bubblegum that didn't belong to me, since that's just what seems to happen to the bottom of women's bags.

"I think I have some work I need to attend to," I said, attempting to conceal my disappointment by shoving things around in my tote.

"Aha. Here it is!" I said triumphantly, as I hit my elbow against the sidewall on the upswing.

The phone flung from my hand, slapped Shep's seat, and shattered as it hit the floor. The glass cover cracked into tiny pieces, but the phone remained intact.

Shep stood up and picked the phone up off the floor.

Could I be any more embarrassing? I blushed uncontrollably.

"It's okay, it's just the cover," he said. "It's not damaged."

"*Damaged,*" I repeated. I hated that word.

* * *

"It doesn't make sense," I asserted. "How can one be good and yet lack integrity? It's not possible."

Mother stood at the kitchen sink, feverishly scrubbing the stubborn residuals from her favorite cast-iron frying pan. I sat at the kitchen table, sipping vanilla-bean coffee.

"It is. Don't you know the meaning of *integrity?*"

I confirmed with a nod, though I was lying.

She continued. "It means being one and the same on the outside and inside."

"Still doesn't make sense," I said. "If your actions are 'good' on the outside, then aren't you 'good' on the inside? Aren't your external actions indications of your inner self?"

"Indications, maybe, but indications are not enough to fully mirror a person's soul. Your father was a good man. He was good on the outside. Good in his actions, mostly. But on the inside, on the inside, his intentions were questionable. He anchored himself to his fears and mistakes. His truth didn't mirror the truth. He was damaged."

I shuddered. My father, *damaged*. How a person could be compared to a piece of equipment, like something you could trade in or throw in a dump somewhere, didn't sit well with me.

***

"Thanks," I said to Shep, as I took back my phone.

CHAPTER TWENTY-ONE

HEIRLOOMS

Shep's rusty blue pickup truck was parked outside the train station next to a 25-cent newspaper, comics, and lemonade stand. "I'll take one," he said to the gap-toothed entrepreneurial Girl Scout behind the stand.

Grinning from ear to ear, she said, "That'll be 25 cents."

I couldn't help but grin along with her.

Shep smiled at us both. "I only have twenties. How about you give me a dollar back and we call it even." He pulled a money clip from his tuxedo pocket and handed her the twenty.

"Really?" she asked, her eyes bulging with delight. "Thank you!"

"Want one, Lanna?" he asked.

"No, thanks. I'm okay." I shook my head.

He took a sip. "You're missing out," he said, guzzling the lemonade from the foam cup until it was empty.

I smiled at his goofiness, and we both walked through the lot.

When we reached his truck, he opened the door and lifted me into the passenger's seat. I didn't need his help. Actually, it hurt. But I thanked him anyway.

There were a few run-down stores on both sides of the tracks: an antique store, a used bookstore, and a vacant deli.

I kicked off my shoes and rolled down the window. He started the engine and we took off down the road, my hair blowing in the wind behind us.

We passed a local church with a lit-up sign that read "Come As You Are" and several small nurseries with local flowers, fruits, and vegetables. It wasn't long before my stomach rumbled, and I asked if we could stop at a tomato stand on the side of the road.

He pulled over and I eagerly jumped out. "There's no cashier," I said, looking around.

"What do you need a cashier for?" he asked, pointing at the small, almost illegible cardboard sign that read "$1 per heirloom" and the wooden box sprinkled with dollar bills and change sitting next to it.

"That's crazy!" I replied. "You mean, people don't just come by and steal everything?"

He laughed. "Well, no. There'd have to be people around here in order for that to happen." I laughed back, and gripped the ripest one I could find, finally settling on a tomato the size of a softball. Ready to sink my teeth into it, I looked back up at Shep.

"Want one?" I asked zestfully.

"Why the hell not?" he responded, unable to resist my enthusiasm.

I groped a few juicy suckers, took a pause, pulled a couple of bucks from my pocket to throw into the box, and then went back to searching for the most desirable tomato I could find.

"This one looks good," Shep said. He picked up a small one and swiftly hopped back into the truck.

"That one?" I said. "That one is going to be hard as a rock. Don't you know your tomatoes?" I winked and lobbed a better one over.

He pulled a few napkins from the glove compartment and we sat together alongside the road, slurping and chomping on our heirlooms.

Sunset turned the sky into a rainbow of red, orange, and yellow hues, and we laughed at ourselves and at the sticky mess we had created. When we finished cleaning up, Shep revved the engine and we drove off. Shortly after, the sky transcended into a deep blue, and I was greeted by the familiar glowing blue Moon.

"Hello," said the Moon, smiling from within the night sky. "It will all be made clear soon. Don't be afraid."

"Whatever you say," I said, under my breath.

"Did you say something?" Shep asked.

"Oh, no, it's nothing," I laughed, embarrassed. "I talk to myself sometimes. It's just something I do." I shrunk into my seat.

"Don't worry. I do, too—all the time," he said. "The Moon's beautiful tonight, isn't she?"

I smiled back at the Moon. My heart fluttered. *Maybe you're right, Mrs. Moon,* I thought, watching his eyes shimmer in the light.

CHAPTER TWENTY-TWO

BEAUTY CAN GROW FROM ANYTHING

After a few miles along a dirt road, the night air grew chilly and damp, and we jerked down a narrow path, slowing carefully through thickly settled woods. The farther we drove, the more wild the lush vegetation, the icier the air. Leaves scuffed against the windows. Bugs smacked against the windshield. The Moon teased us as though it were a child playing a game of hide-and-seek, ducking behind the forest trees, and peeping out to spy on our whereabouts. Then she disappeared completely, and Shep and I were suddenly alone in abrupt blackness.

I clenched the sides of my seat, shivering, and I stuttered, "I'm freezing." The vent continued to yield a steady stream of frigid air, despite how contentiously I fumbled with it. Annoyed, I finally put a hand on Shep's shoulder, and asked if he could stop to turn on the high beams and if he could please help me with the heat.

"I'm sorry. I can't," he said genuinely as he braked. "They don't work."

"What?" I said. "You're nuts. This is so dangerous. Why would you escort *anyone* through woods this thick in a patchwork truck that doesn't have heat or high beams?"

Unfazed, he lifted my hand from his shoulder and placed it onto my thigh. "Don't worry," he said. "We're better off in the dark. Bright lights attract unwelcome visitors."

"Or they help you see," I remarked. But for a moment my mind digressed, and I wondered, *is it possible for a human soul to be so bright that it blinds? It does ring true that light attracts unwanted visitors. It certainly attracted my ex.*

"You can have my tux jacket." He reached back and handed it to me.

I threw it over my body like a blanket and fanatically rubbed my arms together to warm myself. A moment later, we were bouncing on the road again. And a few minutes after that, a branch struck through a crack in the upper part of the window and slung at the back windshield, creating a whip-like noise that made me jump.

"Did something hit you? Are you okay?" Shep slid his arm around my shoulder and began subtly massaging my neck with his fingers.

I calmed to his embrace. "I'm okay. It was the sound that startled me. I guess I didn't close the window all the way." I grabbed the lever to the window and rolled it up, but of course it didn't budge.

"I'm sorry it scared you," he said, letting his fingers linger over to my bicep. "Do you think you can find a way to relax? Any detour and there is a strong possibility that we will be stranded overnight. I can tell you from experience, the bears won't bother us, but the insects—they're not what you'd call sexy."

"Ugh. I hate bug bites," I said as I swatted at the mosquitos. "Is there a faster way? You know, one we can take on *real* roads?"

He laughed. "Me too. We'll get there. Just relax."

I cowered in my seat. I wanted to relax. I wanted to feel safe. But I was in the dark. I was in the dark about who I was, and where I was going, and it was the sort of darkness that made the little voices in my head warble like rapacious opera singers. *Maybe my light was born broken. Maybe light is my enemy, and darkness my friend.* Nothing sat right with me. And the growls, flutters, and buzzes of ugly vexations, and their lurking insidious confidants, made me feel not only uneasy but like an outsider in my own skin. *Perhaps I was never as one with nature as I had led myself to believe.*

"Take a deep breath. It works," Shep said, interrupting me from my thoughts. "This next stretch is challenging. This might sound strange, but I need to close my eyes to do it."

He drew his arm away from my neck. "Just trust me," he said, eyes closed, and he began counting.

His actions took a moment to sink in. *Okay, that seems perfectly normal,* I willed myself to think, as I remained silent as a deer in headlights. Well, not quite a deer. That would indicate the absence of an inner monologue. My mind was racing. I sat silently as though I were a slow Loris, a peculiar monkey-like nocturnal primate that covers its bulging eyes with its hands whenever spotted, as though not seeing what it is afraid of somehow makes it safe. *Yes, this makes sense. He'll close his eyes, click his ruby slippers together three times like he's Dorothy in the Wizard of Oz, and when he opens them, we'll be far from the witch and back in Kansas.*

Then logic jarred my brain. "Are you out of your mind? You're freaking me out. I just met you, and now you are going to drive me through the woods with your eyes *closed?* You're crazy. This is not happening. Stop!" I reached for the door handle. "I'll take my chances out there."

He braked and braced me back with an arm.

Oh, shit, I thought. *Now I've done it. I've pissed him off.*

"Cut it out. Calm down. Listen," he whispered. "I know you are afraid. Don't be. Take a breath. Do you hear that bird? The one with the somber whistle. It sounds like a piccolo."

My heart beat fast. I took a breath and listened. "I hear him," I said, my skin crawling with goose bumps.

He continued. "The bird is worried. He doesn't know why I've stopped driving. We're playing a game—he and I. He whistles when it's time for me to turn. *Right* is one whistle, *left* is two; when it's a sharp turn, he whistles low; when it's a 45-degree turn, he whistles high; if he whistles like a dotted line, then he's telling me how much time until the next shift in direction, and the only way I can hear him correctly is when I close my eyes. There's more to it than that, but that's the gist. You have to trust me. Can you?"

Am I a moron? I thought. *Why on earth would I think it was okay to get into this truck with this guy after what happened in the elevator?*

But I nodded. "Okay." I trembled. These were *his* woods. I knew what that meant. I knew what that meant to me.

I bit my lip, resisting the urge to panic, and listened to the woods, as though they and I and he and we were one. I stared into the darkness as though I were home, and let the bird take us away, through the trees, and through my heart.

The numbers Shep whispered were angles and durations, and soon I deciphered the codes with him, whispering under my own breath, softly enough not to be heard but loudly enough for the woods to know that together we were one.

Pausing at each whistle and tuning the wheel to mimic the bird's directions, Shep carried us on.

Yes, I was afraid. But somewhere deep in my spirit, I heard a voice. "You can trust this guy. He is like you. He can see and hear the things that others won't."

I exhaled, and I believed in him. And I kept on believing it. I believed because it was all I could do. Because he had an aura that made him appear incapable of malice. Because he would get me to wherever I needed to be. Because I didn't know where or what that was. He could have harmed me hundreds of ways by now. But he hadn't. What would be his motive to wait?

Unless …

Was he sick?

Perhaps, I thought.

Perhaps we're all sick.

And then I swallowed my fear again and continued assessing Shep. *He has a vibe of transparency.* I had a hunch that most women thought of him the same way. *Maybe that's his trick. Maybe he looks like a man with nothing to hide and that's how he gets women in the sack.*

I trembled. *I must be out of my damn mind.* I gulped back saliva, and forced myself to believe. *I believe that life will take care of me. I believe because I must believe. Because what else can I do?*

My heart beat faster. I tapped my hand against it to comfort myself, though I was careful not to make noise. Then, finally, after what felt like hours, the foliage thinned and the loud beat of my heart turned into a sweet, soft thump, and I sighed in utter relief. The road widened and the light of the Moon returned, and with it, Shep's beautiful brown face and his gleaming eyes.

He turned to me. "I have your back. I promise. I'll get you to Jack safely. I always keep my promises."

As he spoke these words, I nearly began crying, feeling a surge of both love and skepticism. "I doubt that," I remarked.

And then I wondered, *why did I say that to him? Just accept the gesture.* Though, clearly, I was incompetent, and I couldn't. "Why are you doing this, anyway?" I asked dourly. "Did Jack pay you?"

"Pay me?" he replied, puzzled. "That would be silly. No, I don't require payment. I was born into a lot of money. Come to think of it, I could use less of it. What's your favorite charity?"

"What do you mean?" I said, with an air of self-sabotage. "Oh, I get it. You're one of those rich guys who thinks he is too good for money. Okay, rich guy, so why don't we cut through here. There's always something in it for *the man.* It's a network of favors, right? Why not do us both a favor and unload it on me now."

He was silent, but after a moment, he sighed. "There's nothing in it for me. The beautiful feeling of nothing. It feels good to help people every once in a while. That's really all."

"Did he send you to save me or something? Because, you should know, I don't need saving."

"Why would you need saving?"

I hushed.

"You're put together. You look like you have it all worked out," he said.

"It's an act. The right clothes, a little makeup, and a good job—that's the highest honor for a woman in our society," I said. "It doesn't matter if she's a mess inside."

"True," he said. "But it does matter. And we all need saving sometimes. We save each other in little doses. I do a little something for someone. They do a little something for someone else. And that someone else does a little something, until it all comes back around full circle and the whole pie expands."

"I like that," I said, listening, but still feeling exposed.

"Sure, we save ourselves, too, but we don't do it alone, even when we think we're the wisest and most benevolent of beings, capable of immeasurable pain and of superhuman glory."

I shrugged and made a face. "Who thinks that?"

"Everyone," he said. "So, see? You're more put together than you think. There's mess inside and mess outside. Knowing it's there makes you smarter. It makes you ask questions. What's true? That's all there is to it. And I—" he trailed off, and paused.

"You sound like my sister. And you what?"

"Well, I guess, please don't take this the wrong way. I wanted to meet the woman who designed the brilliant billboard ads for the Music Hall in City Square, for no other reason than I liked them."

I blushed. "You did?" I asked.

"Very much so. Jack shared one of your prints with us. He is enamored with your art. He never stops boasting about it."

"He does?" I asked, embarrassed. "Why?"

"Why not?" he smiled. "It's so deep and evocative. I was swept away by it. I thought, perhaps this person gets it. She gets something about how I am that many people don't seem to get. She doesn't just connect the dots; she verifies what's between them first, then she connects them."

I blushed. "Stop toying with me," I replied. "Why are you really doing this?"

He quieted. "I am helping because I want to. Why does it matter? Isn't that what friends do? Help each other? Must everything always be so transactional? Can I tell you something, Lanna? It's personal."

"You're not going to admit to committing any crimes or anything, are you?" I said. "Because that would make me your accomplice."

"No, no, it's nothing like that."

"Okay. Go ahead."

He took a deep breath and exhaled, as though he needed to find courage in himself. "I was engaged once, but one day, out of the blue, my fiancée said, "Shep, you ask 'why' a lot. I like that about you. It's a strong quality. You're very analytical. But I want to make sure we're marrying for the right reasons. The trouble with too much 'why' is that sometimes it distracts you from seeing 'what.' Don't let the 'why' stop you from experiencing the 'what.' Then she did something I'll never forget. It was dark and we had finished making love. I was still inside her, with my head resting on her shoulder." He took another deep breath. "She asked me what color her eyes were, and I asked her why."

"Please tell me you knew what color her eyes were," I responded.

"They were light brown with a greenish tint. I said they were *medium brown*."

"Close enough," I said, knowing that the slight difference between those two shades was the difference between a flower bud and its soil. "How could you not know that?"

"I did know what they were, but in that moment I didn't see her, not really. And not because the lights were off, or because I didn't know her well enough, and I assure you, I have perfect vision. But because, as the son of a hotshot geneticist, I wanted to be recognized for my intelligence, so I arrogantly asked 'why' and it distracted me from 'what' actually makes a person smart."

"And what's that?" I asked. "What actually makes a person smart?"

"Exactly. *What.* As in, what do I see? And what is true? And what does experience tell me? What does this woman, who wishes to marry me, need from me above all else? I could have said any number of things that were true. I could have told her that it didn't matter what color her eyes were because I could see the sweetness of her soul and that the way she thought about the world was what I loved about her. And that's the type of man she deserved. The 'what' she was asking for was love. But instead, I asked 'why?' I questioned her intentions, which meant I couldn't see her, and possibly, she couldn't see me either. She broke it off with me on the spot."

A chill ran over me. I slipped my fingers through his hand. "I understand," I told him. "I'm sorry it didn't work out between you two." I gazed up at the Moon. The stars twinkled. I wondered if I had become so callous that I too could no longer see the essence of kindness, despite how strongly I yearned for it. Was I, like most human beings, too busy rationalizing every detail that I could no longer see 'what' was right before me?

"It will all be made clear soon," the Moon beamed. "Trust me."

I leaned my head against the window and for a while thought absolutely nothing. Sweet, sweet nothing.

We reached an open pasture of swaying yellow daffodils. My eyes fluttered and then shut. Shep played with my fingers in his hand. "It's okay, you can sleep," he said. "Just a few more minutes and we'll be there."

Daffodils, such a lovely flower, I thought. *Yet, poisonous in the bulb.* How such beauty could grow from poison is something I often pondered.

Beauty can grow from anything, even pain …

I closed my eyes. Shep squeezed my hand.

CHAPTER TWENTY-THREE

NOT A BEGGAR

I woke to Shep unlatching his door. He jumped out into a harem of flickering fireflies and rounded the corner to escort me out from the passenger's seat.

In a haze, I sat up, rubbing my eyes and slapping my cheeks to jar myself back into reality.

"We're here, Lanna. Wake up." He opened my door and reached in to help me out. "Welcome," he said, guiding me out of the truck.

"What?" I asked, confused. "This is prison?"

The structure before my eyes resembled a membrane encased in crystal and stone. It was like a greenhouse made from fine crystal china that someone had planted into the dirt and covered in ivies.

He smirked. "To some people."

"What does that mean?"

He shirked the question. "Handy will meet you at the door."

"Handy? Who's Handy?"

His smile disappeared. "He's a friend of your dad's. Hasn't Jack told you about him?" He scrunched his eyebrows, confused.

"Jack never tells me anything," I said, disgruntled.

"Hmmm. Well, don't fret, Handy is good people. I'll see you later."

I grew unexpectedly hurt. "You're not coming with me? It's the middle of the night."

He came back around the corner, hopped into the driver's seat, started the engine, and stuck his head out the window. Smiling, he said, "Don't worry. I'll be back. You're in good hands."

The truck purred and zoomed down the road. I looked at my feet. Then it struck me. "But my shoes!" I called out, chasing after him. "My shoes are in the truck!"

The truck hummed, until it disappeared high above the hill into the field of daffodils.

"Shit!" I hung my head. It was too late. He was gone; gone with my favorite pair of stilettos and my comfy flips. I turned back, and paused to look up at the Moon.

"Why do I always listen to you?"

The Moon laughed from within the night sky.

This is definitely not prison, I thought, my heart still beating fast from chasing the truck up the road in the dark.

A few wide mosaic stairs led to, in my opinion, a rather ordinary entrance, given the paradoxical complexity and unusual effortlessness of the structure.

I walked up the stairs to ring the bell.

While I waited for someone to come to the door, I pressed the wrinkles from my slacks, ran my sweaty fingers through my tangled hair, and stretched my hamstrings.

What time is it? I looked at my watch.

1:47 a.m. I prayed that someone would answer the door.

I chimed the bell again.

After a few minutes of waiting in the dark, I thought about curling up into a little ball and spending the night on the front steps.

I sat down next to the door, trying to get comfortable enough to spend the night outside.

A chill ran over my body. As I rested my cheek at the front door, a thought came to me. I thought of Jack, alone in a jail cell.

"I can't do this," I muttered to myself, crying, feeling vulnerable and alone in the dark without my shoes.

The Moon pulsed. "Yes, you can. Get up off the ground and push that door open!"

You're right. I took a deep breath. *Get up, Lanna! You're not homeless. You're not a beggar. Get up!*

I stood up and pushed the door. It was heavy at first, heavier than I expected, but it widened quickly, and I stumbled in.

CHAPTER TWENTY-FOUR

A HANDY MAN

Inside the room, a handcrafted Persian rug lay perfectly flat against a wide-planked, quartz-like floor. A large pair of wine-colored men's loafers sat next to a baby-blue velvet chaise.

I heard footsteps and saw the beginnings of a crotchety old man emerge. I braced myself for a new encounter. I was in Jack's domain, after all. Nothing surrounding Jack was ever easy, this ambiguous visit included.

Unsure of my demeanor, and my surroundings, I did what I could do to appear non-threatening. I was sure that whoever was there to greet me could easily confuse me for a beggar, though the well-thought-out form of my grubby New York attire still gave me a bit of an edge. At the same time, I hadn't asked for this visit. I had been invited. So, really, the expectation of my arrival should have been somewhat clear, provided I was supposed to be here, and not somewhere else.

The man approaching was tall and thin, and stood bent over with what looked like an aching back. He wore a pair of classic blue jeans and a torn-up cowboy hat. The prominence of his height grew with him as he came closer.

Our eyes instantly met, and I knew it was okay. I got the sense that he was expecting me. But I was not ready for the familiarity I saw in his face. There was a sort of finesse and wisdom to it. He had thick laugh lines around his mouth. What I mistook for crotchetiness had actually been grogginess. He reminded me of someone I had met once, someone uplifting, someone with gravitas. But I couldn't pin down whom.

I extended my hand. "I'm—I believe you know who I am."

He tipped his hat and reached for my hand, instinctively correcting my lackadaisical handshake. "I do," he said.

I examined his face. Everything from his bone structure to the way his corneas shifted from a shimmery green to a deep brown all at once seemed familiar.

"Do I know you?" I asked.

He nodded. "Name's Andy. Friends call me Handy. I am a lifelong advocate of your father. We have much to discuss."

"Oh, okay," I responded, still unable to identify how it was that we knew each other.

I ran my fingers through my hair. It was beginning to soften. My bladder, on the other hand, was begging for relief. "May I use your bathroom?" I asked politely.

He nodded, and pointed. "Washroom is there. Take your time."

"Thank you," I said, and casually walked away.

In my peripheral vision I spotted an eerie black-and-white photograph sitting on the table by itself. I decided not to look at it, instead continuing onward to the restroom.

As I walked, I reflected on the drive through the woods, and on Shep—how he had so calculatedly counted and rotated the wheel. *Left to right. Left to right. Left to left.* And with such unusual precision.

In hindsight, it was poetic and alarming at the same time. I also, for some reason, couldn't shake the feeling of abandonment. How strange it was that I'd already grown attached to my peculiar escort. I wished I hadn't. I knew it was too strong a feeling too soon, something which had never worked out well for me.

I snuck a backward peek at Handy. He was still waiting in the lobby, watching as I walked.

Simulating the lack of boundaries I had experienced the day before in the elevator, I asked myself, *what if this is another unsolicited life lesson?*

I pivoted, choosing to walk with my back facing the wall. If the indignation I had experienced were to teach me anything, it would be that being safe was a priority.

I flexed my tummy and squeezed my fists tightly. If someone were going to attack me, at least I would see it coming.

Handy's voice saddened. "I'll be in the library," he said to me. "You'll see it."

My instincts are off. He's just an old man, I thought, and began feeling sorry for him.

This is not a game of Clue. It is not Handy in the Library with the Candlestick. Or was it? A woman could never be too careful.

CHAPTER TWENTY-FIVE

CRYSTAL LIBRARY

It was a photo of a perfectly plump baby boy wrapped in a pashmina. He was crying, and I could not deduce from his facial expression whether he was in joy or in sorrow—perhaps it was both. I carefully put it back down. The eerie black-and-white photograph I had noticed on the way into the bathroom was not that eerie at all.

I stopped snooping and continued toward the library to meet Handy.

My vision started to blur. A haze of cigar smoke had crept from the farthest corners of the hall, probably where Handy was waiting.

There were candies placed in ornamental bowls along the wall to the library. I popped a piece of butterscotch into my mouth and played with it with my tongue until it stuck to my back molars. Stopping to loosen my jaw and unstick the candy from my mouth, I noticed the ceiling.

In the ceiling there was a carving of a rotund naked woman cradling a weeping garden snake. It was delicately carved, so much so that the intricacy would have gone unnoticed had I not been standing there picking my teeth like a baboon.

The naked woman, a healthy-looking woman, held the snake adoringly into her chest, comforting it as though it were her child. The tears from the snake's humanlike eyes shattered into a mosaic of blue glass, as though the artist himself had accidently dropped a wine goblet there, and rather than sweep it away, chose to embellish it. Then the glass extended, forming a long arrow to the place from where the billows of smoke were growing in size.

I followed the arrow to its end, where theater drapes swung in a sea of harsh burgundy.

Water splashed and a wooden wind chime clunked.

My heart began beating fast.

I pushed through one of the drapes and cautiously stepped into the enormous cloud of smoke.

There was a tree growing from the center of the room through an earthy hole in the floor. Its branches wound and bent gracefully upward, as though it were stretching its arms up over its head to relax.

Above it, a magnificent crystal skylight composed of tiny triangular glass panels shed rays of electric starlight into the room. The glass panels were lined in copper, and I could see through them, straight into the sky above.

Beside the tree, an indoor koi pond extended to its roots. The room had been built on a brook. The pond ended in the room and disappeared under the floorboard, most likely continuing somewhere in the wilderness that surrounded the house.

I childishly took to the floor. Some unfiltered part of my soul decided that crawling was a suitable way to explore. My knuckles and knees scraped against the crevices of the slate stone flooring, and though it hurt, the pain felt right, as though some pain were necessary in order to fully absorb its pleasure.

I shuffled whimsically toward the winding tree, splashing my hand in the pond, and finally settled beside a mosaic glass engraving in the floor that said "LIBRARY."

Handy was sitting in a soft baby-blue armchair, peacefully puffing on a pipe. Beside him sat a black globe, a half-eaten watermelon, a large telescope, and a filthy wooden box. When the smoke cleared, our eyes met.

"Like it?" He smiled, amused.

I slid my nails through the engraving, pretending to draw the words with my fingertips, and nonchalantly responded, "It's okay." Then, after a moment of pause, I said, "It's beautiful. It reminds me of the cavern by Mother's cottage.

Have you been there? I haven't been there since I was a child."

He grinned. "I know," he said, refilling his pipe. "Everyone said it could not be done. But I knew. I gave them the space to create. Told them they could do what they liked, but that it had to be on this plot of land. I trusted them, I believed in them, and the Divine gave us this."

I smiled sarcastically. "Who are the Divine?"

"You have to work with what you have, young lady, not against it," he smirked, evading the question and casually relighting his pipe. "I have a proposition for you, *Miss* Zar. You are a 'Miss,' correct? You are unattached?"

I rubbed my eyes and frowned at the smoke. "Why do you do that? Don't you care about whomever you're attached to?"

He extinguished the pipe.

I looked away, up through the ceiling and into the stars, into the cosmos.

"Do you have the non-disclosure agreement?" he asked.

"Yes," I nodded, and reached into my tote. "Here you go." I handed him the document.

He took it, and his eyes scanned to the bottom of the page where I had signed.

"It is settled, then," he established, and set the document aside. "We've arranged a room for you here. Enjoy the grounds. Think of this as home, except—"

He raised an eyebrow, ensuring my attention.

I submitted.

"We have one important rule."

"What is it?" I asked.

"It may confuse you."

"Oh, goody, I'll add it to the pile."

"The pile?"

"The pile of existing confusion."

"Well, you are in the right place," he replied. "It is an oath of silence."

"Of silence?" I said, stunned.

"You won't understand."

"Try me."

He continued. "But you will."

I sighed. "Go on."

"You may speak through your gestures. You may speak through your heart. But you may not speak with your vocal cords."

"But why?" I blurted. "What is this about?"

He continued. "It is hard to understand at first. Everyone feels the same way. But, believe it or not, you will grow to appreciate this rule. I promise you."

"I hardly know you," I responded. "Why should I trust you?"

"Yes," he replied, searching my eyes. "That is an important question. But the more important question is 'will you commit?' "

"I'm not sure," I replied, conflicted. "Commitment and *committed* like to play cruel tricks on me, if you get my drift."

He laughed. "It's a commitment to yourself. To see the universe with fresh eyes."

"I don't understand," I said. "I assumed the contract was for what I might see in Jack's prison. What happens if I *need* to speak? Will I be silenced?"

He smiled. "Then speak."

"Okay, sure," I said anxiously. "None of this makes any sense to me."

He smiled. "Good. Then you are on the right path."

"And what about Jack? When will you bring me to see him?"

"Yes, Jack, of course. When will you be ready?"

"Ready?" I repeated, knowing that contentment was far from my heart's grasp. "If you don't mind, can we please do it later? Tomorrow? Or the next day?" I looked down at my toes. "It might take some time," I said, embarrassed. "Is that going to be all right?"

"My dear, you're welcome to stay for as long as your heart needs. You'll see him when you're ready," he replied.

I grew slightly less uneasy. "Okay, thank you," I said. "For being so—" I paused. "Kind."

After a short time, Handy rose to show me to my room. I insisted we remain in the library. I had never been in a room more stunning. He happily complied, and carried over a yellow chenille blanket. I wrapped it around myself and then scooted onto what looked like a Japanese sleeping mat.

He returned to his armchair, read a book, and fell asleep.

Lying there, I stared up at the crystal ceiling, at the bending tree, at the stars. It felt strange, like I was camping, only inside. I did not like the no-speaking-out-loud rule. Nonetheless, I believed that being a guest in one's home had certain requirements and obligations, and, like I always had, I resolved to act within the boundaries of my host's wishes. As long as it wouldn't cause harm.

Shep slid a drape aside, stepped into the room, saw Handy sleeping in his chair, and started stumbling. He had changed out of his tuxedo, was freshly showered, and was wearing a pair of flannel pants and a sweatshirt.

"Pssst, I'm over here," I smiled, waving him over, euphoric to see that he had returned.

"You came back," I said, relieved to have him near.

He pulled a mat and a blanket from a stack of mats next to mine and plopped them onto the floor. After hopping in, he wrapped an arm under my shoulder. "I love this place," he said. "Plus, I didn't want to leave you in the dark."

I smiled. "You smell good," I said, melting into him.

"You do, too. Your hair smells delicious," he said, kissing my head. "Coconut. Mmmm," he mumbled, and fell asleep.

I wanted to sleep, too, but all I could think about was the uncanny new rule. It was an interesting challenge. But the thought of being stuck with only my own thoughts, well, would anyone want to be stuck with my thoughts?

I stayed on the mat awhile, but the adrenaline of the day lingered. I replayed the nauseating elevator experience over again in my mind.

An old man I hardly knew had molested me, and the stranger who had softened the indignation was now sleeping beside me, and, just like that, I was putty in his arms.

What this place was, what it would do to me, and how it would lead me to Jack all remained questions. I prayed that I was not completely impervious to joy. I prayed that I was safe. I prayed that I was on the track to something better.

I knew that *somewhere* within me—the same somewhere I had tapped into via art and nature—existed the capacity for true happiness.

I thought about the many enigmas of nature: the irony of meat-eating plants, and lizards that change color to blend into their surrounds. I thought about all there is to discover and how we, as a society, so rarely know what we think we know. I thought of the ways in which confusion allows for discovery, for innovation, for invention.

"Stay open," I told myself, praying for the intoxicating feeling of being small again in a very large, undiscovered, expanding universe.

And yet, the questions I held in my belly about my ability to identify love scared me. I could not empathize with myself. I did not like feeling so vulnerable, so dependent. I did not appreciate the many failures of my love life taunting me into believing the unthinkable: that I was damaged.

CHAPTER TWENTY-SIX

WANDERING EYES

Sometimes in life there is no way to reduce the flame of insomnia, I thought, after lying on the floor in the library for some time. *Let it burn.* There was no use trying to sleep. I rolled to my side and up onto my feet, careful not to wake Shep. I set off to explore my surroundings.

Handy's head kept falling forward in his chair. He was snoring, and startling himself awake. Before I left the room, I grabbed a couple of pillows and blankets, and tucked them around his body so that he would be warm and his neck more comfortable. It was slightly invasive of me, but he was old, and I felt badly for him.

The sconces that lit the hallway provided enough light for me to poke my head into different rooms without bumping into things. Each room had its own obvious purpose. One room was filled with musical instruments. It was, clearly, the music room. Inside it displayed everything from a didgeridoo, to bells, to a Steinway piano, and there were other instruments, too: a flute made of jade, a Tibetan singing bowl, and drums from all parts of the world.

Another room was filled with yoga mats; another was an indoor greenhouse. There were many greenhouses, in fact. Some filled with unusual flowering succulents; others with strangely potted potato plants; and an empty one with just one flower, not a particularly pretty flower, just a white, orchid-like flower with a half-broken stem.

That's me, I thought. *A bland, lonely flower.*

Foolishly, I had assumed that I would be alone during these deep nighttime hours. Instead, everywhere I went, I was met with glowing eyes. Green eyes, blue eyes, hazel eyes, black eyes. All with stories to tell. Only, they didn't.

One gentleman had a hand that was missing its index and middle fingers. I felt sorry for him. But when his hazel eyes lit up, I knew there was nothing to feel sorry for; he was a happy man.

When it came to mouths and lips, I found I was shy, much shyer in the quiet than I ever felt through words.

My body tingled. My heart pounded. I was alive.

I was looking at a display of Middle Eastern antiques in the den, when I felt an unfamiliar presence behind me.

I turned to see who it was. A woman wearing a headscarf stood staring at me from across the room. Light cast shadows onto her face so that I could not make out her features clearly.

I moved toward the fireplace and fumbled for a couple of pieces of wood.

Her stare did not weaken. In fact, it seemed to intensify.

With one piece, I fed an already zealous fire. The other, I held close to my chest.

The fire snapped and crackled. The heat swelled.

The woman glided out from the corner into the light of the fire. Her brown eyes sparkled. In the darkness, her spidery lashes and bushy brows had cast unseemly shadows onto her face. In the light, she was attractive.

She picked up her thin rectangular reading glasses, put them on her face, and then handed me a daffodil.

How pretty, I thought, and I dropped the other piece of wood beside me on the floor and reached for the flower.

Thank you, I nodded.

She sat down on the sofa beside the fire, smiled, and patted the space next to hers, inviting me to join.

I plopped down beside her.

"Follow me," she said with her eyes, and she took a deep breath, followed by another and another. I mimicked her deep breaths, inhaling when she inhaled and exhaling when she exhaled. After several deep breaths, I finally released myself of all the thoughts that were swimming around in my mind. My thoughts had turned into colorful neon fish. But when I reached out to touch them, they vanished.

I giggled. She did too.

CHAPTER TWENTY-SEVEN

GOODNIGHT, LADYBUG

"Shep, is that you?" I could not see his face, only the outline of a body lifting me. The smell of cedar-wood aftershave lured me into the warmth of his arms. My body, exhausted from sleep deprivation, melted into the strength of his biceps. I mustered a hand upward to reach for his face. I wanted to feel his cheeks.

"It's all right," he said. "I'm bringing you to your room." His eyebrows furrowed like fuzzy caterpillars between my fingers.

"Where were you?" I murmured. "I was searching."

"I should ask the same of you," he whispered.

My eyes drifted in and out of slumber. My body swayed like a sailboat anchored to a dock; the water so calm, the anchor rendered unnecessary.

"Will you stay with me?" I managed to say.

A door creaked and I lifted an eye open. It was still dark, but the light from the Moon shone through the window just enough for me to see the contents of the room: a heavy wooden twin bed with a lacy bed skirt, a flickering firefly, a night stand, a tall wooden dresser.

He set me onto the bed. The gravity of my body against the mattress sent me into heaven. I rolled onto my side and snuggled up with the soft woolen blanket that he covered me with. He ran his hands through my hair, down the side of my face, down my neck and shoulders, and across my belly, stopping when he reached my navel. He kissed me on the forehead and whispered, "Goodnight, Ladybug."

I melted to sleep.

Twenty minutes or some unknown duration later, I woke.

"Wait, what did you call me?"

Then I fell back to sleep.

CHAPTER TWENTY-EIGHT

THE SNAKE OR THE EGG?

The woman's name was Setara. Her eyes dazzled under the self-selected confines of her own stylish headscarves. I wondered where she was from but did not ask. It would take too much effort. Wherever it was, it was far. Maybe at some point, when I understood how to engage more fully, I would find out.

She had met me in my room that morning with a basketful of clean white towels, handmade soaps, razors, a toothbrush, toothpaste, fresh underwear, and a beige linen dress embroidered with purple flowers. I rarely ever wore underwear, and still had the spare in my purse, but I figured it was time to start, at least for the time being.

My nonverbal questions and words were met with quiet smiles and peculiar gestures, each more mysterious than the last. I gratefully took the basket and sat it on top of the bed. I was very hungry, and I didn't want to shower until I had some food in my belly.

Salivating over the thought of what I imagined would be a delicious breakfast of bacon, eggs, and farm-fresh produce, I nudged Setara to take me to the kitchen, where I was disappointed to find very little protein.

She looked at me, baffled.

I pointed to a plastic crate inside the refrigerator, flapped like a rooster, and oinked like a pig. "Meat and eggs. Where can I find them?" I was saying under my breath.

"Ah." She nodded at my request, reached for her car keys, and gestured *follow me* with a wave.

I followed her into the driveway, where her hunter-green sedan was parked around the corner, underneath a carport made from fig trees.

Upon seeing the figs, my heart skipped a beat. *What if she takes me to Jack?*

Suddenly, I lost my appetite and panicked. *Please don't take me to him; I'm not ready.*

Setara smiled, took hold of my hand, and gently pulled me into the garden. She sat me down under a myrtle tree.

I closed my eyes and breathed a sigh of relief. The whooshing of the winds lifted my hair and massaged my shoulders. Again, as I had beside Setara the night before, I inhaled the wind until the regular rhythm of my own breathing gave way to a sort of peace. Like the long-handled wash brush that dangled on the towel rack inside my shower, my breath could relieve the itch of old wounds. It couldn't heal, but it could clarify.

I opened my eyes. Setara's eyes seemed clearer, browner. "Thank you," I said aloud, knowing that if ever there were words to say aloud, they were words of gratitude.

"Thank *you*," she said softly, with an accent that I did not recognize. This was the first time I heard her light, airy, and slightly off-pitch voice. I could tell she was the sort of woman who sang aloud, even when it was not the proper time to rejoice. There was incongruence to her voice; it was grating and yet appeasing.

She stood up and pointed to a bird's nest high above our heads. Pulling me up to join her, the little light bulb in my brain lit up.

Above us, a group of baby bluebirds were hatching from their shells. We watched as one cracked through and toppled over into a gooey mess of excitement. The babies' mother fluffed her butt on top of her newborns. She whistled a poignant tune and at times fluttered above her babies, simply to delight in her accomplishments.

Somehow, the frazzled cries of newborns and their mother's soothing whistles melded together into a colorful harmony, loving and full of wonderment. It continued on this way, with each sibling cheering for one another and their all-knowing mother tweeting angelically beside them, until suddenly a hawk flew overhead, and the sweetness of their song warped into horror. The mother cawed and her feathers tufted. She hopped protectively on top of her fledglings. Her babies' cries grew more anguished. The hawk circled, its scissor-sharp claws swooping at them with an ugly voraciousness as it lunged upon them.

My heart raced. "Stop that!" Rushing to find something, anything, to ward off the hawk, I grabbed a thick fallen tree branch and charged it at him.

The hawk took notice. The branch distracted him briefly. It retreated high above the nest, but without hesitation, it swooped back down. The mother cawed. A fledgling tripped. An egg reached its tipping point and fell over the side of the nest.

Not believing that I could reach it in time, I closed my eyes as I scrambled to catch it. *What are you doing? Open your eyes, stupid!*

Cowering to my knees, my eyes clenched, the distraught cries of the mother and her babies emulsified into an earsplitting wind.

"Come find me!" I reached into the sky, my soul crying for help.

Suddenly the grass parted and a garden snake emerged. And, just like that, the hawk vanished. The crying slowed. All grew quiet.

Setara pat me on the shoulder. I didn't look up. She nudged again at my side, jolting me out of hiding. Her bright eyes were beaming. Gingerly, she inched open her headscarf and presented its contents. There lay the egg, unscathed.

I hung my head in relief and fell to the grass, laughing. I laughed and laughed. Taking the egg out from her hands, I twirled it between my fingers to examine its blue exterior and oblong brown spots. I kept laughing. When the laughter began to settle, Setara wrapped an arm around my shoulder, gave me a funny look, and began rubbing her belly.

Here's the breakfast you asked for, her eyes were saying.

I was red with embarrassment, then pure shame. *I may be hungry, but I am not a predator,* I thought. Yet, I was left with a question, an idea. *A snake can be a predator or a savior, depending on the moment. Can't we all?* Then it occurred to me: some snakes are never predators. Sometimes they are misclassified. Sure, they may smell fear, but it's what they do with it that counts.

She smiled at me as though she had access to my thoughts. *There, there.* She patted me on the back. We rose, and headed toward the house to find a tall ladder.

The mother bird chased after us, but somehow she knew this baby would be okay, so she returned to comfort her other needy babies.

When we found Handy asleep under the tree in the library, Setara tickled him awake, and he huffed furiously at her. I showed him the egg and his eyes instantly lit up.

I stopped craving bacon and eggs that day, at least in the conventional sense. Instead, I began craving the warmth of family. Recalling only a handful of childhood days, before the trial, before the loss of my father, before the world came crashing down, I wondered whether I ever possessed the same warmth within my own family that I had witnessed with the birds. I sensed I had, but I could not figure out how to get that feeling back.

CHAPTER TWENTY-NINE

CONSCIOUSNESS AND NATURE

Each sunset, the crystal mansion fell into a rip-roar of activity, lacing my depression with layers of curiosity, in spite of what felt like emotional confinement. Familiar and often friendly faces appeared, distracting me from my worries, and yet feeding them too.

With every encounter, a few unplanned, yet perfect by design, handful of visual cues wove together into a bouquet of personalities. I made up lives for each person I met.

I often found myself voyeuristically peeping into the estate greenhouses to watch the men study the unusual botany germinating behind the glass walls.

Throughout the day there were sessions of light stretching, followed by long, sometimes tedious, bouts of heavy breathing. No one cried in the silence.

No one but me.

Sometimes they held me. Sometimes we all laughed together.

How could I know nothing about these persons and yet feel I knew everything? I thought. *And what do they think of me? What can they see that I can't?*

Gazing through the window at a striking gentleman in a white overcoat, I wondered, *who are you in your real life?*

He smiled and invited me in. I rejected the invitation. He shrugged.

I remained silent for days, and so did the others. We were united in silence. The men preferred it, even when it seemed words were the right way to communicate.

I envied them. Their capacity for kindness and comfort in solace far surpassed my own. Who were these perfect souls who emitted lightness in such a heavy world? My thoughts wavered between meaningless and painful.

Were they all liars? Liars playing an exquisite game of make-believe, a game designed to trick the brain from experiencing reality, a game designed to prevent true feeling from emerging? Were they stowaways running from the truth? These questions made me fear them.

My instincts stung and sent me meandering out of the house. In the haze of a purple and yellow night's sky, my loneliness elongated. My mind twirled ceaselessly in a merry-go-round of unanswerable questions. I glided along the ivies, obsessed with the intentions of the keepers and sleepers of the house.

I summoned the Moon. It shone starkly, as it always did. "This way," it said.

At the edge of the yard, where the landscaping ended, tall, prickly grass began. Up on the horizon, the daffodil field glimmered. I slithered toward it.

The grass was dry and coarse, and splintered my skin. Yet I could not harm myself under the light of the Moon. I could not harm others. Only in awareness could I create grievances against those who cared for me. Without awareness, with distance, I was absolved from harm, justified in my paralysis. Perhaps that was why Handy prescribed such silence. Had my father undergone the same process?

My sadness erupted. I leaped into the thistly grass and dug my hands into the dirt. Cool air filled my lungs. I ran through the grass like a pronghorn antelope escaping the piercing sound of a shotgun.

I ran freely, without reserve, slowing only to swat the crickets perched on leaves and to caress my own silky skin. I ran and ran until I reached the field.

The luminescence of the daffodils sharpened with my lightness. I could hear them, just as I had nights before, swaying in the wind, playing their music for me.

I was lost in their song. Butterflies ate my stomach. I dropped to my knees, winded. I sat in the field, relishing the freedom of being somewhere and nowhere.

Something fluttered. An army of bats obscured the light of the Moon. The music stopped. I heard whispers—whispers that hovered like ghosts through the air. Whispers filling the space around me with the warm, tingly sensations that only whispers can.

"Who's there?" I said, my heartbeat picking up pace.

Two stones clanked, as if to strike a fire.

I jumped and whipped around. "Who's there?"

I heard the sweet cry of a newborn baby.

No, it couldn't be, I thought.

Fear washed over me. *What if it is?*

Then I lost my mind. I swept my hands across the daffodils, frantically shoving the flowers aside. I surveyed the land with my ears.

In nature, I could trust only my instincts. The cry grew farther and then closer and closer, until it was very close.

I gasped and jumped aside. *Something whisked my ankle and darted aside. A raccoon? A coyote?*

Shivers ran down my spine. I held my breath, waiting for whatever it was to make its next move.

"Meow," a cat hissed. "Meow."

I released my breath. "Strange place for you to be, kitty," I said aloud, reaching out to pet it. "You scared me."

It nuzzled my hands with its wet nose and nibbled my toes playfully with its pointy teeth.

"Ouch," I said, kicking it gently aside. "What are you doing so far from home, anyway?"

Out of the darkness, Shep's blue pickup rounded the corner. The truck stopped in the driveway and Shep popped out. He paused and peeked suspiciously into the yard. He threw the truck door shut, recoiled at the sound of metal on metal, and vanished into the house.

"Meow," the cat answered, caressing my leg erotically.

"Stop that," I said, laughing and shooing it away. "Would you like to join me, kitty? Someone is looking for me. I should head home."

The cat followed behind as I rushed back to the house, only to disappear moments before the field ended. "Kitty?" I called. "You coming?" But all I could hear were crickets.

The wind picked up. The freedom I had experienced earlier only felt like loneliness again.

Where the wind had earlier pushed me into the field, it now fought viciously against me. I forced my way through it, returning through the landscaped yard, passing the rounded driveway and up to the mosaic stairs.

I paused at the heavy front door, breathless. I rested briefly and pushed the door.

Damn, it's locked!

I headed to the greenhouse door around the back and knocked, and the man in the white overcoat let me in. This time he smirked at my muddied appearance. I was covered in mire.

I walked cautiously to what appeared to be the closest washroom, a room I had not yet explored, and flipped on the light. The air smelled floral. It came to me as an exaggerated pleasant surprise, though it should not have, since it matched the floral interior.

The room was quite lovely. It had an attached sitting area with two Victorian sofas and two armchairs, both upholstered. The sofas were plush and hand-stitched in blue and gold fabric. There was a standup shower with a crystal skylight, similar to the one in the library, though proportional to the shower, and a small wooden stool. Next to it there was a separating door to a low toilet. All of the walls were embellished with dainty hand-painted lilies.

I smiled and flailed around the room like a tipsy symphony conductor, but halted my whimsy with the premonition that someone was watching me.

I frisked myself, making sure my body parts were still intact. My awareness returned. I no longer accepted that my presence in the crystal mansion was of my own choosing. With certainty, I knew Handy was connected to Jack. That something about his elegance, his aura, was pure, and that Jack trusted him. And there were other peculiarities—the way the mansion was designed: the carport made of figs and the library that resembled the cavern by our cottage. Jack would no doubt realize that I would see the connection, the resemblance between these things and things that I loved. *But could I trust Jack? What was the meaning of this visit? Was this his way of redeeming himself?*

My father was capable of immense harm. He was responsible for death. For the destruction of families. Lives. I shivered. *What happened to that boy who was once my friend? Was he the man from my dreams? The one whose eyes had been replaced with black tar?*

And so it went that fate and open-mindedness, together with my impenetrable fascination with humanity, my unsettled hormones, and my daring desire to find love, obliged me to trust in the silent unknown. Though part of me wanted nothing more than to quit, I was too coy to excuse myself from this journey, this collision, and was struck by the notion that fear and risk require exploration; that truth only finds its way into viewing when faced; and that life is a myriad of opposites. I had found a gentleman, a Sheppard in the wild. It seemed only fair that I should find a criminal too. But who was I to judge? And who was the criminal and who was the gentleman?

Whatever my father had done, I knew I was born to discover it. What could an old man do to me now, anyhow? I was probably more likely to create harm for myself. I probably already had.

I was not a religious girl, nor did I think myself a pious or righteous one, but in this moment I was compelled by a pull so strong that even my own reflection appeared to move toward me in the mirror.

I put my face up close to it, looked deeply into my own shimmering navy eyes, and summoned a higher power:

"God," I said. "If you are up there, give me the grace, serenity, and clarity to survive this; the intelligence to seek the truth; and the open-mindedness to accept whatever will come of it."

I sat down on the lavish couch in the sitting area. *What a relief.* I thought of the cat in the daffodil field. The fear of an abandoned baby morphed into the sweet music of a giggling one.

CHAPTER THIRTY

DISGUSTED EUPHORIA

Several weeks passed and I had not yet seen my father, though more and more, elements of the mansion reminded me of him. I questioned whether I could ever face him at all. It would be like looking directly into a black hole. *Would I lose myself?*

I wanted to see him, to learn his version of the truth, and yet the thought of looking him in the eye repulsed me. Would he expect me to embrace him? Would I be expected to reciprocate a love for him that I was not sure was there? Would I have to throw my arms around him and grovel with adoration? Would I have to perpetuate the lie that I loved and missed him? How could I do that—I didn't know who he was. I had learned that the hard way. Time and time again.

I wanted to scream. I wanted to tell him how much he had hurt me by leaving us, by leaving Mom. How watching her love the idea of a man, a father who wasn't there, had made me believe that every person, be he a sinner or a saint, was worthy of my affection, my love, my being. And this made me hate him more.

And then I imagined us hugging. I imagined closure. And that made me happy and sad all at once. I felt gross and elated, disgusted and euphoric. I wanted to call him a weasel, a criminal—the kind of man not even God would love. I wanted to tell him to his face.

But when I closed my eyes and breathed, he wasn't a criminal. He was a person who deserved a chance. Twenty years of letters and checks had given him that right. He loved me and I had once loved him. It was I who was stuck. I couldn't see past the past, and the amorphous future riddled me. I didn't want to see him bound. And I knew I'd be unable to protect him, to free him.

And so I did not ask to be taken to him. To the prison. Or to wherever he resided. And the members of the house understood without my saying so. They let me be. And Shep, who had been there with me all along, grew somber watching me slip further and further into a deep sadness, and night after night he held my hand while I cried and ran into the field, until one night he didn't come, and I fell asleep alone in the daffodil field, and when I awoke, the daffodils were covering my body, protecting me from the heat of the morning sun.

I cleared away the bugs that had come to sleep with me and rose to return to the house. I could not recall a morning when I had not unexpectedly stumbled into someone who resided or took refuge in, or tended to, the house. The house was always alive, always breathing. But today, I saw no one.

A thought came to me. It was the thought of losing Shep.

I retreated to the library. The serene geometric glasswork of the ceiling lit the room like a kaleidoscope. Suddenly I felt sicker than I had in all the days preceding this one. I didn't want to be alone.

Isn't there someone to whom I belong? Someone who belongs to me?

I wanted him with me.

Tears filled my eyes. I could no longer hold back the growing love within me. I didn't want to run from it. I didn't want to hide from it. I hid it from anyone who gave it to me. Mom. Mary. Setara. Handy. Jack. Shep.

Shep was the most compassionate man I had ever met. He sought nothing from me, and it brought him peace and me a sense of calm. It was a joy like no other. I didn't want to hide anymore. Not from my colleagues or from my boss. I was tired of suffering. Tired of being alone. Plain old tired.

"I give up," I whimpered, still feeling the pressure to hold it together. "I don't want to feel this way anymore," I told myself, fighting to let go. "I give up," I repeated. "You can't choose whom you love. You can choose how to love. You can choose to receive it. And that's all! That's all there is! There's no special formula."

Over and over, I uttered these words, and little by little, I unraveled. With each utterance, the weight lifted. At first the words fell from my mouth in a pathetic dissonance of rapid staccatos. I was suffocating.

"This is my fault. I did this. This is my fault. If I hadn't run away that night. If I had just told Mary to stay. If I had listened when Mom told me not to go to the brook … " I swayed back and forth, rocking rhythmically, holding myself, crying, and letting go.

With each inhale, the words "I'm sorry" filled my lungs. I squirmed in agony on the slated floor. Then, gradually, the air inward found a way outward. Through some deep well growing from within me, stillness emerged.

It crescendoed, vibrating over my being in a wave of revelation. My limbs tingled. A sensation of deep relaxation washed over my chin, out of my fingers, out of my toes.

I am not alone, I told myself. *I am not alone. I deserve to be loved. Open your eyes, Lanna. What do you see?*

My body loosened. My tears stopped. My cheeks no longer stung. I no longer felt shame. I was present. I was alive. I was safe. And I was done suffering.

I stood up slowly, rubbed my eyes, and smiled. I walked over to Handy's blue armchair and thought about him sitting there, puffing on his pipe, and how fearful and awkward I had been when we first met. I laughed, thinking of how I had walked with my back toward the wall, afraid some maniacal evil would attack me. He looked so sorrowfully at me then. How silly it all seemed now.

I plopped down into his chair, laughing at the thought. And yet my belly still ached.

Strange. I noticed that Handy had left his yellow straw cowboy hat on the side-table next to his pipe.

I picked up the hat. Under it, a yellow sticky with a note that read "This hat and these articles belong to your father. He wants you to have them" sat on a stack of photographs, newspaper cutouts, and magazine articles.

I flipped the hat over and looked at the tag. It read "Sugar."

Strange, I thought again. *How bewildering it is that something that belonged to Jack could give me a feeling of comfort.* I flipped it onto my head.

I shuffled past the articles, straight to the pictures. I recognized the people in them but only in that way a person might recognize someone whom they once sat next to in a dark movie theater, or a couple sitting next to your table at a romantic restaurant.

I shifted back to the articles and began reading.

A Progressive Approach to End Recidivism in the New Age of Genetics |*Science & Philosophy Magazine*| Pg. 7

The Andrew Yates Oates Foundation, in collaboration with the Department of Agriculture and the SEEDs of Life Foundation, is funding a new project designed to give outlaws and prison inmates, specifically, individuals of unfortunate life circumstances, a second chance, provided they carry residuals of a special gene, dubbed by renowned geneticist Landon Sheppard as the "farming gene."

These lucky gene-carrying participants will surrender themselves fully into the care of Andrew Yates Oates, who has made special arrangements with statewide lawmakers to donate a mind-boggling 10 billion dollars toward the new Bulldogs' stadium.

The donation will generate economic growth in three states, with projections of 13 billion year over year.

The "farming gene," according to philosophers, anthropologists, and geneticists, may be linked to an unusual culture of prehistoric man, known for withdrawing from hunter roles. Religious and philosophical texts reveal that carriers of this gene are believed to have fled traditional societal roles in pursuit of farming and agriculture.

Ancient historical texts indicate that gene carriers may contain high levels of a hormone known to foster unprecedented levels of philosophical thinking.

According to wall drawings found in caves around the world, these farming philosophers often died through suicide or by social persecution.

However, there exists speculation that small subsets of gene carriers forged rather progressive and joyous lives, particularly when they were able to find an agreeable man or woman to cohabitate, germinate, and farm alongside them. Curiously, only a handful of these gene carriers exist today, several residing in prison.

Scientists, gurus, and businessmen alike hypothesize that carriers of this gene, provided they are young enough to probabilistically succeed in societal reconditioning, may not only be capable of adapting new behaviors, but may indeed carry a natural, unique rapid-response innovation hormone.

At best, the program lends itself to the progressive end to poverty and famine for all mankind. At worst, the experiment is a profitable investment for corporations, a determinant to the public with the loss of hefty tax income, and a dangerous criminal endeavor.

Psychologists refer to numerous research studies on sociopaths as prime examples of dangerous and severely impaired individuals, incapable of adapting to society, with disastrous consequences. Sociopathic criminals are cited as the primary candidates for rehabilitations gone wrong. Such sociopaths typically are said to be "born evil," having been responsible for countless serial murders throughout history.

Accordingly, the Oates Foundation will not allow carriers with sociopathic tendencies to participate in the program. To date, none of the participants exhibit sociopathic tendencies, but rather, the opposite—they have intentionally fallen into lives behind bars as the result of a sort of self-imposed punishment for low-level crimes committed. Traditionally, the district attorney would have turned a blind eye toward these types of crimes. This is one of the arousing peculiarities that set gene carriers apart from typical offenders. Moreover, during extensive scenario-based neurological testing, gene carriers responded with amplified feelings of remorse in the frontal cortex of their brains. Where sociopaths feel none and ordinary people feel some, gene carriers feel more than their share. Some neurologists say, "It is as though these offenders are carrying the burden of remorse for all humanity."

Independent women's organizations argue that the project unfairly over-values the abilities of men over women with the same genetic makeup. Logically, women's roles in society naturally lent themselves to the farming and agricultural space.

In response to this outcry, the Oates Foundation has issued a statement of sincere apology:

"While we wholeheartedly support the endeavors of women, and believe these women's organizations are correct to make the above assertions, the historical renderings required to convince lawmakers to support female submergence into the program are, unfortunately, inconclusive. We will fight to resolve these issues as amicably as possible."

Starting Monday, September 18, 1989, the participants, whose names shall remain anonymous, will take refuge in the care of Andrew Yates Oates.

The Oates estate has been a topic of interest for many reporters and architects, as no one has yet been able to determine its precise whereabouts. Card invitations to the estate by former guests have been auctioned off at upwards of $300,000. The city of Chestnut will be hosting a celebratory event in honor of the launch of the new program.

MISSWIRED by Tara Makhmali

August 3, 2010 | *The Daily Sentinel* | Obituaries | D5

Ngyuen Azurite, age 31, born in London, England, to mother Victoria Terrance Vãn and father Tu Vãn on April 4, 1979, passed away on July 28, 2010, in the town of Azalea, Tennessee. Mrs. Azurite graduated summa cum laude with a Master's of Business Administration from the London School of Economics in May of 2009. She married Sam Azurite on July 5, 2009, in Cambridge, England. Nguyen is preceded in death by both of her parents, and is survived by her spouse, Sam, and their newborn son, Vãn Azurite. The Azurite family asks for privacy at this time.

MISSWIRED by Tara Makhmali

June 22, 1988 | *The Chestnut Reporter* | Crime | E7

A 40-year-old man from the nearby town of Chestnut, New Jersey, was arrested Tuesday for the alleged murder of husband and wife Nico and Sophie Azurite. The man was apprehended in his home, several blocks from the scene of the crime, where neighbors say they could hear him arguing with his family. The suspect is also facing allegations of domestic abuse.

MISSWIRED *by Tara Makhmali*

September 18, 1989 | *The Chestnut Reporter* | Local | A5

One year after the grisly death of Nico and Sophie Azurite, Jack Zar has been sentenced to 15 years in prison. The verdict comes as a surprise. Local opinion on the outcome of the Azurite case remains conflicted:

"I've known Jack a long time. This is inconsistent with his personality. He cared deeply for people. Something isn't right."
—Wu Lee, College Student

"I don't know if Jack did this crime; I didn't see him much, but I always suspected he was capable. He was a weird guy, always scribbling pictures of mold into his notebook. Mold? Who likes mold? Heck, I'd seen the way he looked at Nico's wife, always trying to help her and such. If he was trying to help my lady that way, I'd show him a thing or two, weird as he was, that's for sure."
—James Stevens Frank, Restaurant Owner

"Nico killed Sophie long before Jack ever could."
—Gin Su, Neighbor of Deceased Couple

"A man at odds with his own soul suffers, regardless of his earthly punishment. Whether justice is with or against him is only as relevant as his ability to repair and heal his suffering soul."
—Andrew "Handy" Yates Oates, Philanthropist Billionaire

"The DA is sending a blunt message to citizens that violators of the Gun Law Safety Act will be punished without mercy, regardless of who they are or what their good intentions. If Mr. Zar had used common sense to notify the authorities, Nico and Sophie would be alive today. This is what happens when citizens take law enforcement into their own hands."

—John Kelper, Partner Kazath Law, Politician

"They're wrong. Jack's a nerd with a big heart. So he gave her a gun to protect herself. So what? That doesn't make him a killer. You ever meet Sophie? There wasn't a man in town that wasn't curious about that woman. Jack's only mistake was that his intrigue naturally led him toward the things no one ever wants to look more closely at. This wasn't his fault. He's a martyr, not a criminal."

—Moz Zane, Neighbor of Zar Family

CHAPTER THIRTY-ONE

GUT CHECK

I dropped the stack of newspaper clippings, dizzy from information overload.

Was my father a gene carrier? Was he a program participant? Where was he? Would I even know what he looked like if I saw him? Where am I?

My heart felt weak and powerful. The weakness, I cradled into my belly like a hungry child escaping the cold, only to find there is no food inside. The power, I harvested like a father in hunt.

Then, out of nowhere, I had a memory of my mother's sweet voice. She was saying, "Listen with your head; forget your heart. Sometimes you're wired wrong."

Sometimes, I huffed. *More like, always. Okay,* I told myself, *be nice to yourself. Listen to your mother; listen with your head.* I picked up the stack again and plowed through the publications, starting with *The Reporter.*

June 22, 1988, *The Chestnut Reporter, Crime* – A 40-year-old man from the nearby town of Chestnut, New Jersey, was arrested Tuesday for the alleged murder of husband and wife Nico and Sophie Azurite. The man was apprehended in his home, several blocks from the scene of the crime, where neighbors say they could hear him arguing with his family. The suspect is also facing allegations of domestic abuse.

I scowled. *This is a lie. These are lies. We were all together in the hospital because of Mary. Because of what I did. Because I pushed her down that ladder.* Why is this article written this way? Jack was not arrested at Mother's cottage. He wasn't at home. He didn't abuse us. I shed a tear, now believing that I was "the" lie that had persuaded the jury. My anger had spoken volumes to the jury. The six men and six women, the way they had looked at me. "Look into a child's eyes and you shall see the truth; we all think as adults, don't we?" But Mary's injury, the cut on my cheek, I did that. Those were my fault, and I had convicted my father long before the world ever could. I flipped to the next piece.

September 18, 1989, *The Chestnut Reporter, Local*: One year after Nico and Sophie Azurite's death, Jack Zar is sentenced to 15 years in prison.

Eyeballing the opinions, nothing struck me. Then, there it was. Handy.

> "A man at odds with his own soul suffers, regardless of his earthly punishment. Whether justice is with or against him is only as relevant as his ability to repair and heal his suffering soul."
> —Andrew "Handy" Yates Oates, Philanthropist Billionaire

My God, I thought, and I dropped the stack, took a breath, picked it back up again, and thumbed onward. There was no date in the *Science & Philosophy Magazine* article headline, but it hit me as I read.

A Progressive Approach to End Recidivism in the New Age of Genetics, Science & Philosophy Magazine: The Andrew Yates Oates Foundation, the Department of Agriculture, and the SEEDs of Life Foundation fund a new project for outlaws and prison inmates who carry a special "farming gene" ...

Starting Monday, September 18, 1989, the participants, whose names shall remain anonymous, will take refuge in the care of Andrew Yates Oates.

I thumbed back. September 18, 1989. The day of my father's verdict and the start of the new project—they were the same day. *September 18, 1989.* My heart raced. I went on to the next piece. Something didn't add up. *Who was Nguyen Azurite?*

I reread the obituary. Next to it, there was a picture of a baby boy.

"Nguyen is preceded in death by both of her parents and is survived by her spouse, Sam, and their newborn son, Vän Azurite."

I recognized the little boy in the photograph. He resembled the baby from the picture I had seen on the table by the washroom near the entrance of the crystal sanctuary the night I arrived.

PART FIVE

PART FIVE

CHAPTER THIRTY-TWO

SLITHER

Sam was sitting at his walnut desk, drinking aged scotch and thumbing through a stack of stolen library books, when a note popped out from one of the books:

To My Wealthy Thieving Friend,

Given the types of books that you are reading, and the manner in which you are borrowing them from the library, I took it upon myself to add this journal to your conquest. It may benefit you (and the library) for you to work through your personal issues. I expect you to return or refund the library for the titles for which you so kindly donated.

Your friend,
Fred the Librarian

P.S. In case I have not made myself clear, I know it is you, Sam. You've been stealing from the same rack for years. Investment bankers need not rob from thine own stash! Use the journal!

Embarrassed, Sam began thinking it is a bit weird that a wealthy investment banker would be stealing the same teenage horror novels he donated to the library years ago.

He stared at the blank pages of the journal. Its emptiness taunted him, as if it knew.

Dammit, Fred is right. I have to face this.

Sam enjoyed reading horror fiction books as much as he imagined all women enjoyed reading InStyle magazine and getting their nails done. At least, those were Nguyen's guilty pleasures.

It wasn't the gore or the guts that he liked. He usually skimmed past that. He liked the books for their endings—the likable victim escaping his tormentor, finding a new nest to call home, moving forward in life as though no trauma or wrongdoing had ever occurred. There was an element of hopefulness to it.

Investment bankers are not thieves, they're bankers!

He smirked. Okay, maybe they're a little of both. The irony was not lost on him.

A garden snake emerged from the earth. It shimmied through the grass, swam through a pond, slithered up a tree, and clung to the window.

Sam picked up a red pen. NGUYEN, he wrote at the top of the page. Suddenly, he was overwhelmed. The memory of losing her made him furious. He took it out on the pages, shredding through them with the sharp tip of his red pen.

In all the ways he was capable of hurting, he never imagined she would be one of them. His stomach sank. Nguyen, he thought, as though speaking to her directly. If you can hear me, I miss you. Please come back. Give me a sign.

He dropped the pen, crying, and began pressing the pointy ends of the pages into his fingerprints. Some of his nails had dirt beneath them and some were jaggedly cut. The enormity of his hands made them hideous.

I have the ugliest hands, he thought. But she loved them anyway.

A ray of sunlight bounced from a mirror on an adjacent wall to another mirror nearby. Through the hanging glass, he spotted his reflection. Looking at himself, he felt shame.

He stepped back, finally noticing that a snake was clinging to the window.

Their eyes met. "What are you doing here?" he said to the snake, as he rose uneasily to meet it at the window.

The snake's eyes dilated. "You're afraid," it said, hissing, its tongue whisking the glass. "Everyone carries their fear somewhere. Hssss. Why are you afraid?"

Snakes smell fear. Be calm, he thought to himself. "I'm not afraid," said Sam cautiously, his chest pounding.

Again, the snake hissed. "I smell your fear. Why are you afraid? Why do you suffer?"

Vän Junior called out from the living room. "Dad! Where are you? I fell off my bike! Can you fix it? It hurts! Ouuuui! It hurts!"

The snake retracted to the top of the tree and hid in the leaves.

"I hurt myself. Look." Vän pointed to a gash on his knee.

Sam stayed at the window.

"Dad, what are you doing over there?"

Sam hesitated. He looked at the bloody scrape on his son's knee. "Looks bad. May I have a closer look?" He patted his lap, instructing his son to climb atop.

Vän was a perceptive boy. He saw what his Dad hid, including his permanent sadness, which often confused him. Yet, in no time at all, Vän's expression flipped from confusion to conviction, and he plunged forward, grunting, scratching, clenching, and clawing, until he made his way snuggly into his father's lap.

Delighted with his son's tenacity, Sam joked, "Which leg?"

This angered Vän. "Daddy, it's right there. Don't you see? There." He pointed to the blood gushing down his shin.

Sam latched his hand around the scrawny leg, lifted it to his lips, and kissed an area near the wound. Mwah.

"Ow" said Vän. "That hurts! Why'd you do that?"

"Sorry," he said, pausing. "I only did it to make you feel better. You know, Son, if you think your pain is bigger than it is, it will hurt more than it has to."

Vän's face grew bewildered. "Uh," he responded, kicking forward for momentum, jumping from Sam's lap and bolting out of the room.

Kids. Sam shook his head in disappointment and then shuddered at the mere thought of rubbing alcohol. It would probably sting, and Vän would cry and be angry with him for cleansing his wound, but it was the only way to prevent infection. This spurred an epiphany. He picked up his pen and calmly jotted his thought into the journal.

"Forgive me, Ngyuen," he wrote. "The cruelty of this life without you is intolerable. Yet, it must be tolerated." Then he flipped the journal shut, searched for a place to store it, and shoved it into the back of a squeaky dresser, behind a stack of old pocket squares.

The garden snake poked its head out from behind a branch, intentionally smacking its tail against the window to create a large thud.

Their eyes met again. "Are you still afraid?" it asked.

"Boo!" Sam juked. "Scat!"

CHAPTER THIRTHY-THREE

BIRTH

Setara called out to Handy. He was already there with his toolbox. He wanted to wrap himself around Setara. He wanted to tell her it would be okay. But there was no time. There was a time to embrace and a time to throw emotions aside and move faster. He pulled the torch, wrench, and hammer from his toolbox and started removing the car door.

As it cracked open, Nguyen's limp hand slipped out from the underside of the door. Blood slid down her dainty polished fingers.

Setara kneeled next to the door and slipped her hand under the woman's hand. Handy focused on removing the door. The rain pounded. It fought against them, several times extinguishing the torch.

Setara's heartbeat intensified. She was unfamiliar with this level of adrenaline. She had spent her life avoiding chaos, meditating the days away, perhaps in preparation for this moment, this day, this particular variety of chaos. The rain hid her apprehension.

Finally, the door loosened. Setara prepared to move the unconscious woman out of the truck. Handy grunted and heaved the door away. Setara lifted the woman out from the truck, sliding their two bodies in tandem.

Though Nguyen lay unconscious, Setara could still see the ripple of contractions cascade over her body.

The rain calmed. "You're safe," Setara whispered into the woman's ear.

A beam of sunlight crept out from behind the clouds. The woman rolled to her side.

Handy reached for his phone, ready to call his emergency medical team.

The woman's eyes twitched.

Setara wanted to jump up and slap the phone away from him. "No. This woman is already in active labor," she protested. "We have to help her do this. There's no other way. Go to the house. Bring the Arnica, ice, and an IV."

Handy fled into the field.

Quivering, she whispered into the woman's ear. "You're okay. My name is Setara. It means 'star,' but today, you're the star, and we're going to pull you through. You're doing a great job."

Fifteen minutes later, Nguyen regained full consciousness and cried out for Sam. "Where is he?" she uttered. "The pressure. I want it to end. I want him out. I need Sam."

"He's coming," Setara assured her. "He'll be in your arms soon."

Handy returned swiftly with the supplies. A great bolt of motivation overcame Nguyen. She used it to hoist herself up onto all fours.

Setara rubbed the ice and Arnica on the woman's back. The cubes melted over Nguyen's body like lava. A few minutes passed. Nguyen pushed the baby out into Setara's arms and it let out a cry. Setara immediately placed him onto Nguyen's bruised chest. She held him with what little strength she had left.

"He's so beautiful," Nguyen said, tears rolling down her cheeks. "You're strong like your grandfather, little angel," she whispered to the winds.

"We have more work to do," said Setara.

Nguyen nodded. Her eyes dimmed.

"Give me one more big push."

Nguyen pushed.

Setara's heart sank. Something was not right. "You're going to feel a pinch," she said, pulling at the umbilical cord until the placenta slid out of Nguyen's battered body.

CHAPTER THIRTY-FOUR

THE EMERGENCY CREW

Sam stumbled out of the emergency helicopter, picked himself up, and ran like the wind to his wife and newborn son.

The wind whooshed. In the distance, Nguyen could see Sam's glimmering blue eyes as he charged toward her. A ripple of peace waved over her body. Finally, he had come. The light of the sun warmed her cheeks. Their tender baby slept safely with his tiny ear pressed to her heart, calmed by its irregular beat.

Sam dropped to Nguyen's side and grazed her cheeks with his lips. He pushed her hair away from her face and caressed her arms. Kissing her, he let his fingers linger over her deflated body. His soul warmed to the mere sound of his infant's breath. Had there ever been a more magical sound? He watched as the baby's chest rose and fell, and fell and rose. He gazed longingly into Nguyen's weary eyes. How beautiful they were. Why had he never noticed?

But before he could tell her, Death stole the light from within her as though by accident; as though its fountain pen had burst and black ink had spilled through her veins by transactions miswired and credits reversed. In her face, he saw flashes of his mother all over again, and he became a boy, hovered over a limp body covered in blood and pressing his head against her wet breasts in search of a beat.

Then there they all were—the emergency crew—fighting to resuscitate Nguyen and insisting that Setara hand Sam's delicate infant over to them for examination.

The baby wailed.

"No," Setara argued firmly, knowing Sam was too lost in his own grief to discern the right thing to do. "He can't start life this way." She looked at Sam with compassionate eyes and instructed, "Take off your shirt. Place this boy on your chest. Let him hear *your* heart."

And Sam knew, like few others would ever know, that to search for a heartbeat that isn't there is a pain that no child should ever have to experience, and he tore through his collared shirt, took the naked child from Setara, came to his knees to a sitting position, and cradled his boy. Setara twirled her shawl around them and dropped to her knees beside them, while Handy rushed to hold them as tightly as he could. Together they hummed a song of glass chimes that altered the air. It let the baby rest, and the crew too cried.

CHAPTER THIRTY FIVE

ALPHAGREEN INVESTMENTS

Sam adjusted his power tie into a double Windsor knot. He smoothed aside a cowlick. He swiped his fingers across both bushy eyebrows. He lifted a piece of lint from his custom-fit charcoal suit, and he secured his opal cufflinks.

He needed a haircut, but the sleek way he styled it, along with his bronze complexion, made his hair length corporately acceptable, and his blazing blue eyes made him downright mesmerizing.

He leaned back into his chair. The board meeting was at 2 p.m. His stomach churned. *What am I talking about?* He took a deep breath and threw his arms up into the air as though he had just run a marathon.

Okay! It's a Board day! My goal is to listen—to understand. I've always earned my power that way. By listening, and making them feel heard and respected.

He calmed down, trying to refocus his attention on the research he had gathered for the meeting.

The door opened. Tre, Sam's assistant, entered. "Hey, Boss, the Board would still like to meet with you at 2. Should I confirm?"

Sam nodded. "Yes, thank you, Tre. My calendar is up to date. By the way," he asked with mild aversion, "is that a new eyebrow ring?"

"This? No. I got it a month ago. The tattoo is new." His eyes bulged with excitement as he lifted his T-shirt to show off the Mandarin symbol chiseled into his right pectoral.

Sam laughed uncomfortably. "Wow, that's great, Tre, I like it." He hesitated. "What does it mean?"

"I have no clue," replied Tre. "I just liked the lines." He remained exposing himself.

Sam laughed. "You mean, your abdominal lines?" He gauged Tre's reaction. Nothing. He tried again. "You know, Tre, if I ever meet an Asian man with an English tattoo who doesn't know what it means, I'll buy you a drink." He grinned.

Tre looked confused.

"Okay, Tre, never mind. Thank you." Sam put his hand on his head. "Please put your shirt back down. I don't want to get a notice from HR."

"Oh, yeah, I meant to ask you. Jenny from Employee Relations wants to know how you're doing."

Sam considered smashing his head into his desk but instead ground his teeth into a dry grin. "Tell her I'm great, and thanks for asking. Now please shut the door on your way out."

After Nguyen's death, Sam's jokes didn't elicit the same level of laughter he was accustomed to. This was to be expected for a while, but in recent years, journalists had added to his troubles by taking an interest in his misshapen life, sensationalizing some of the more gruesome facts about his childhood.

First they leaked that he was the orphaned son of a horrific double homicide. Then he was the orphan who had survived the foster-care system. At sixteen, he lucked out when an entrepreneur and owner of a line of nail salons and dry cleaners took a liking to him and hired him for his body mass and the cheap labor. She let him take home the clothes that no one had come back to collect, and out of the goodness of her heart, covered his college application fees.

Nguyen's death coincided with his success in the financial markets, and even people who did not know him acted reverent, suspicious, and sorry for him. His jokes, of course, were never particularly funny, but as far back as college, people at least laughed when he laughed. For reasons unclear to him then, they were drawn to him.

He wasn't unaware of his looks. He did have to use them to his advantage to swindle a bed (or, wink, more) for the night, usually from co-eds with self-esteem issues, which he understood all too well. It wasn't ideal. He wasn't proud of it. But college debt nearly drove him to suicide. How could a man without family go from zero to negative? He merely did what he had to do to survive.

It was while he was matriculating into his post-graduate program at the London School of Economics that his female Indian professor of Macro Finance looked at him and said, "Well, dear, you're beautiful and as tall as the Shard. You're bound to be a newsworthy CEO. I do hope you'll shape up in my class, or you'll ruin the world for all of us in it," and he realized just how profoundly his looks would shape his destiny. At a whopping six foot, five inches, he towered over most of his peers.

Her remark was both kind and cutting. It was unfair of her to target him in that moment; there were many smarter students neglecting to pay attention in her class. But her words stayed with him, and he began logging social cues as though they were math formulas, comparing reactions based on physical attributes, ethnicity, and race, and he discovered that what she was saying was, in fact, true. Yes, he would eventually be responsible for a great many people and his decisions would have an impact. The thought of ruining the world resonated, and the strategic use of his height and mind became a duty, and after losing Nguyen, he realized, a burden.

Now social interactions had returned to mostly stark, uncomfortable silences, often concluding with a concerned "How are *you* doing, Sam?" to which he would reply, "Great! Busy as usual!" and move on.

An occasional pep talk from a well-meaning novice gave him a smidgeon of optimism. But even when this kindness found its way into his ears, he questioned whether the altruistic act was an honest act or simply another form of narcissism, the sort he found prevalent in corrupt organizations that launched charitable giving foundations, but then had no qualms pilfering from the retirement accounts of the elderly and those in need. He knew his stature and his status made him an asset and a liability. And that his every move had to be meticulously planned and carefully controlled.

OK, the Board, the Board, the Board. He rose from his swivel chair and suavely glided to the dry-erase board full of catchy phrases and annotated formulas. *What's the goal here? Get these guys on my team. Heavy investments in bio-medical research laboratories ...*

We absolutely must remove ourselves from the media. Out of the media, that's key. Don't want our people inadvertently sharing investment strategies, or worse, journalists giving away the names of our top talent. If we fuss over our successes, we'll grow vulnerable to our opponents. We cannot be vulnerable.

Two p.m. came quickly. He got up out of his chair and walked to the corner of his office to gaze out at the City. His reflection in the window gave him pause.

He returned to his desk and picked up his personal notebook, which he signed and dated every day. On his way to the boardroom, he stopped at his secretary's workstation.

"Tre, can you please look up the address for every horticultural association in the Northeast? Also, I'd like for you to set up a meeting for me with the author of this article," he said, as he removed a crumpled black-and-white photocopy of an article from his journal. "We need to set up a distraction so the media backs away from us for a while. I think I have an idea. Can you set it up?"

Tre nodded without looking up. Sam thought about cracking a joke, but decided against it, quickly moving along toward the boardroom.

CHAPTER THIRTY-SIX

THE BOARD MEETING

Centennial Investors magazine's gala was a notorious shit-show for wealthy hedge fund managers who used the event as an opportunity to out-snob each other publicly. The Board sat at a large oval table, bickering over exactly who and why. None of the AG Board members wanted to attend, mostly due to scheduling conflicts, but their lead marketer insisted otherwise:

"A sponsored table and accompaniment by a favorable client to the *Centennial* is not a nice-to-do. It is a *must!*"

Sam entered. A hush rotated around the room like a wave of cheering fans giving the ole ceremonial wave at a high-energy baseball game.

Bill Reilly, Board member and longtime friend, jested: "Ladies and Gentlemen, it's the infamous, the notorious, the infectious Mister Sam Azurite!"

Sam laughed and sauntered up to him. "Cut it out, Reilly!"

Reilly stood up and they embraced in fraternal camaraderie.

"Good to see you," Sam replied quickly, preparing himself to sweep the room in a round robin of introductions. He glided to each Board member, diligently prefacing every handshake with their individual name.

Surveying the Board, he sensed his introductions were successful. They all seemed rather pleased and at ease with his presence now. This was important. He had spent quite some time over the years struggling with a faltering memory. It took dedication to overcome this annoying obstacle, which required that he rebuild his internal encoding and decoding neural wiring so that he could regurgitate meaningless information on demand.

As a young boy, he had not struggled with this dilemma, but after the murder of his parents, his brain periodically blanked. In 10th grade geology, Sam recalled anxiously tapping his knees against the desk while his teacher drew pictures of rock formations on the chalkboard, as though it were yesterday.

***

Teacher: "What's this formation, Sam?"

Sam: "That's not a formation. It's a chalk outline of a dead body."

Teacher: "That's not funny, Sam. Study your diagrams."

***

This empty exchange always pissed off both Sam and his geology teacher.

He paused at an empty seat. *Is someone missing?* He doubted himself briefly.

The room had fallen into an uneasy silence. He winked and looked down at his watch. It was 2:15 p.m. He mentally took stock of the members in the room. *I don't think I'm missing anyone,* he concluded. *There is even a guest.* He looked at the pretty young marketer in the flowy navy dress. She was standing patiently in the corner.

He cleared his throat. "Okay, everyone, ahem, let's get started. We can begin with the *Centennial.*"

The marketer smiled appreciatively. "Thank you."

Chuck smirked. "I say we nail this one down right now and send you over there, Sammy-boy. You'll charm'em with those pretty blues of yours."

Sam: "Reilly, who are we courting?"

Reilly: "CocoMedtron, DDS, and SEED"

Sam: "SEED?"

Reilly: "You never heard of 'em? C'mon, Sam, I thought you were sharp." He stretched his arms out to reveal the slender white wrists hidden underneath his banker's cuffs.

Mason: "I'm paired in the same group as the head of Coco at the golf tournament later this afternoon."

RJ: "DDS is weak; let's cut them loose."

Reilly, chuckling: "RJ, you don't care for DDS because of your altercation with their VP. Should've kept your hands off that woman. You knew she was trouble."

RJ: "No, DDS recently made an investment in Blue Torch. I know the technology. It's weak. They're on the wrong path."

Sam: "Reilly, can you have Martha check that out?"

Reilly: "Take that down, Martha."

Chuck: "All right, it's settled. Sammy, we're send'n you to the *Centennial* with the lega-babies."

Sam: "I'm a better golfer."

Chuck: "You're going to the *Centennial*. Bring a date, and I don't mean Tre."

Sam turned to the pretty marketer. "You'll be my date. Can you arrange it?"

"Oh, okay, sure," she replied, noticeably unsure of whether she was being hit on or whether it was purely business.

Sam turned away, grinning. "Reilly too."

Reilly jested, "Gladly! Why, Sammy Az-hole, I thought you'd never ask."

Sam turned his attention back to the marketer. "Thank you," he said. "You may be excused."

They all watched the pretty marketer shuffle swiftly out of the room.

"Now," Sam continued. "We have a lot to discuss. I'm here to listen, but first I have some important requests, starting with quashing this media frenzy we've gotten ourselves into. I have a solution …"

CHAPTER THIRTY-SEVEN

THE GALA

A saxophonist wove the sultry music of Louis Armstrong and Billie Holiday into the twinkle of the New York City skyline. An unlimited array of Prince Edward Island oysters, smoked salmon, crab cakes, caviar with crème fraîche on miniature homemade dill baguettes, homegrown vegetables galore, and a rainbow of delicacies made their way from silver trays into Sam's mouth.

The venue was stunning. Floor-to-ceiling windows and a wrap-around terrace with scintillating views of the most architecturally transcendental sites the City had to offer. The diamond-lit blue-purple-and-green Empire State Building pointed through the sky as though man had played no role in its build and the solar system had reached its mighty arm down from space to anchor it from on high, staking it straight through to the core of the earth as a gift, a compass, an oracle for street pedestrians. *This way*, it would say.

Bushels of blossoming flowers toppled over the edges of every surface with no less allure than that of tantric concubines. Orchids from Hawaii. Bluebells from Spain. Tulips from Holland. Roses from Afghanistan. Each with a perfume that could transport you to your destiny. Windows, tables, and chairs lined in taffeta fabric shifted in color depending on which angle the light hit and where the music took you. Cherubs prancing with bows and arrows next to nude ladies holding porky blue-eyed babies—these were painted into blue-sky ceilings. White-gloved attendants, hired from the Center for the Arts to dance as they served, glided as gracefully as ballerinas; *they were ballerinas*.

With dangling crystal chandeliers that swung gently in a spectrum of glitter and awe, and well-adorned people laughing, and dancers dancing, it radiated a sort of beauty common only to the filthy rich, but appreciated most by lovers, whose hearts, satisfied by the belongingness of one another, saw life in no other way. Sam pined for Nguyen. His heart panged. He had grown dreadfully lonesome.

Reilly handed Sam a drink.

"Oh, good, you're here. You finished the pitch. I thought I would be stuck here alone," said Sam.

"Lonely, maybe. Alone, no."

He sighed. "Is it still that obvious?"

"About as obvious as Chuck Johnson's affair with that hostess over there." He winked. "Isn't it time you had some fun, Sam? We've mourned. We've moved on. You've mourned. Now it's time for you to move on. It's time to have some fun."

"It's not that easy. I can't have fun here."

"Where then, Sam? The boardroom? This is where fun happens. Look at your date; she's a showstopper. You can't find a woman like that on a pole, you know. If you don't take her home, I might."

Sam turned toward his table. His client and his date (the pretty marketer) sat together, engaged in conversation. She caught Sam eyeing her from her peripheral and waved him over. He lifted his drink, saluted her, and declined. "You know how I feel about dating employees."

Reilly pulled an unlit cigar from his tuxedo pocket and pointed a 'hello' to the marketer. She nodded and smiled.

"Join me for a smoke," Reilly said to Sam.

"You know I don't."

A twenty-something photographer wearing Gucci eyeglasses and black jeans popped up next to them. "Picture. Say cheese," she said, snapping the photograph, and glided away to film other heads of state.

Reilly pulled Sam to the door. "Join me anyway. No photographers allowed out there."

A white-gloved doorman opened the door to the terrace. The two stepped out into the warm summer air. A few "lega-babies" stood in the corner, smoking and bitching.

Sam shook his head judgmentally. He despised lega-babies. These were the entitled sons and daughters of wealthy aristocrats. It was not their inheritance that made him disdainful. Fortune was not antithetical to virtue. That part of the equation was a choice, and these individuals were arrogant, reckless, and oblivious. Society rewarded them for it as though they were demigods impervious to the rule of law. In contrast, middle-income Americans, immigrants, women, people of color, and the poor worked diligently and humbly, and had been punished not only for marginal mistakes, but for their noble achievements, too. It was, of course, this outlook that reminded Sam that even in dire circumstances, he was lucky. He was gifted both with presence and with mathematical intellect.

Along the far side of the terrace, a bar made from pink amethyst glowed. Beside it sat several glass tables with light installations, cigar boxes, and hookahs. When a guest puffed on his or her cigar or hookah, the light from the installation cast images into the smoke.

At the other edge of the terrace, an electronic humidification system, designed to resemble a tropical rainforest—wildly messy and lushly leafy green plastic-made plants—separated the smokers from the nature lovers. A rose and herb garden sat on the other side of the humidifier. Within the garden sat a Steinway player piano and clusters of lounging sofa-chairs. The bushes and shrubs surrounding the chairs had been shaved into the shapes of animals. Each animal represented a company sponsor.

One corner of the terrace remained vacant, frill-less, and yet it still diffused a sort of surreal charm. It had been left vacant intentionally so that those who still knew how to take pleasure in simplicity would be granted another present: it was the only spot, perhaps, in all of New York City where a person could still see stars. Sam drifted toward the vacant corner. Reilly nudged him instead to the opposite ledge to sit beside him at the cigar bar.

They settled into their chairs, listening to the honking of taxicabs and jazz piano, and together they peered out at the skyline.

"You see those boxes, Sam?" Reilly asked, alluding to the high-rise office buildings congesting the sky, another form of starlight to some.

A white-gloved server whisked by. "Light, sir?" he asked.

The server sparked his lighter, and for a moment the fire and smell of smoke transformed the two business tycoons from men into boys. Reilly puffed until his cigar was lit.

"Will that be all, sir?"

"Yes."

Reilly continued his train of thought. "Sam, how many boxes do you think there are out there? A billion?"

"Sure."

"That's a billion nobodies just hoping to make it somewhere in this town." The red cherry tip of Reilly's cigar flickered. The light installation from the table nearby transformed his cloud of smoke into the AG mascot: a tooth-bearing lion with the mane of a golden retriever and the splicing claws of a rabid vulture.

"Well, you made it!" Reilly declared, amusing himself with the smoke.

"Is that what they want, Reilly? I mean, really? To blow smoke in the shape of a lion on a city terrace?"

"Aww, Sammy," Reilly consoled. "Lighten up. What do you want? What will make you happy? You have money. Power. There's a woman waiting for you to come inside." He winked. "What more could you want?"

"What do I want?" Sam blurted, the question releasing from his mouth as though for the first time. He held his stomach. "I want to stop feeling like a gutted fish. The mother of my child gone. Vanished. Up in smoke. Like this town of smoke and mirrors."

Reilly placed his hand over Sam's shoulder. "Look at you. Look at where you are. How many orphans would kill to be in your Ferragamo shoes today? They're not here. You are. And the whole *smoky* world conspired to get you here. Trust it. You've got to move on, man."

Sam rolled his eyes. "Let's get one thing straight. The world has not *helped* me do anything. It's been one gutting followed by the next." He spread his arms high above his head and waved them in a circle above them. "This! Sitting here, none of *this* matters. Don't you know that, Reilly? This is the lie we live to keep ourselves distracted."

Reilly smiled. "Sam, people are beginning to notice." He puffed his chest out at a gentleman near the end of the bar who was smoking a blunt.

"Need a hit?" said the gentleman, offering his marijuana.

Reilly waved him off and returned his attention to his candied cigar. "Come on, Azurite. You have to admit this is a little fun. Just a little. Even if there are a few too many peacocks around."

One of the waiters quickly swooped over and whisked Sam's empty glass away. A minute later, another scotch was on the table. "Another," Sam said to the server as he drowned himself fast.

The server nodded and returned with a new glass.

"Are we good now, Reilly? Can we move forward?"

"Move forward?" Reilly rebuked. "You're a broken man, Sam. I'm trying to help you. You tell me. It's up to you. You ever think 'what about Vän?' Ever think Vän deserves to taste life too? Or do you plan to break him in like your old man?"

"F*ck off, Reilly. You are the perfect example of how the world helps me. You preach about life, but you have no concept of what it means to lose. You don't care about your own wife. You barely knew mine and she was my everything." He pointed to his empty scotch glass.

"And *you* let her down," Reilly replied. "So why take it out on me? On your kid?"

Sam continued. "I didn't even know it until she was gone, Reilly." He looked into the empty glass. "What kind of a man am I? What kind of a man doesn't know he loves his wife?"

"The good high-functioning alcoholic kind," Reilly snarked.

Sam reddened. "Waiter, I'll have another."

"Don't you think you've had enough?" Reilly leaned in and placed a hand on Sam's shoulder.

"Bugger off." Sam swatted him away, rose from his seat, darted toward a waiter's tray of refills, haphazardly grabbed another, and nodded for the doorman to open the door.

"C'mon, Sam, don't be this way," Reilly nonchalantly called behind Sam as he hurried off. For a brief second, it appeared that Reilly did indeed have the impulse to chase after him, but instead he stood up from his bar chair and moseyed over to the gentleman smoking the blunt at the other end of the bar. Then he puffed his cigar and giggled at the lions in the smoke.

Sam muttered to himself, "and that is how the world *conspires* to help. So much hype, such little wisdom." He sped past the young marketer, who looked up at him, concerned. He shook her off hastily and whizzed to the lobby to grab his jacket. One of the photographers soared behind him until he reached the coat check.

CHAPTER THIRTY-EIGHT

THE COAT CHECK

"You're not allowed back here." The old lady behind the coat-check counter shooed the photographer away.

"Sorry," said the photographer, and she retreated.

The coat check smiled wryly at Sam. "*No* means *no.* They don't seem to get that they're not allowed back here. The boss," she pointed to herself, "has told them repeatedly. Now, I'm sorry, do you have your ticket?"

Sam fumbled through his pockets. Pulling at the lining in his trousers, the contents of his pockets scattered to the floor, among them his money clip and car wand. He reached down to pick them up, but all at once the alcohol hit, and he missed, instead joining his belongings on the floor in an awkward manner.

The old coat-check lady rounded the corner. Holding back laughter, she reached down to help him up. "Well, that's one way to do it. Are you okay?"

He sat up, dizzy.

She coughed.

"Fine. A little embarrassed is all."

She bent down and held out her veiny arm to help lift him. "Oh, honey, no need to be embarrassed in front of me. Old as I am, I've slipped and fallen once or twice. At least you didn't do it on your own."

He took hold of her petal-soft hand, and then slowly chose to let go. "Mind if I sit here a minute? I feel ill."

The old lady smiled and let go of his hand. She looked down at the money clip and the plastic car wand. "As you like," she said, and returned to the coat-check counter.

A few minutes passed and she appeared with a brown fold-up chair. "Mind if I join?" she said to Sam as he stared off into space. "You remind me of my grandson."

"That's nice," he replied. "I don't have any living elders."

"Pity," said the old lady. "You don't seem that old. What happened to them?"

A sour cramp quaked in his stomach.

"I'm too old to care about spreading lies and sharing secrets," she said, sensing his discomfort. "That's why they hired me, though I do have a great memory, if I don't mind saying so myself."

"You *sure* you want to know?" Sam managed to slur.

"Try me."

"Fine," he said. "My father," his stomach panged again, "killed my mother. Then himself. When I was a boy. No one wanted to have anything to do with me when they found out my inheritance was all debt. I was orphaned overnight." He paused. "I suppose they were right."

"Right about what, honey?" she replied, unmoved.

"I have my father's eyes. He was a drunk."

"Your eyes look pretty nice to me," she said. "Hold on a sec. I have coffee behind the register. Would you like some?"

"You don't sound surprised about me." His head spun as he tried to scan her reaction.

"Me?" replied the old lady. "Oh, no, honey, I've seen and heard it all." She walked behind the table.

After some time, the old woman returned with a large mug and a small pot of coffee. "And you don't look like a real drunk." She sat back in her chair and placed the pot and the cup on the floor. "Help yourself."

Sam lifted the pot. His hands shook as he attempted to pour the hot liquid. He missed the mug.

The old woman laughed. "Stop. You're worse than me." She took the pot. "Hold the mug with both hands. I'll pour."

He held the mug with both hands, as she instructed. His hands still shook, but he was steadier with both hands than he was with only one.

She smiled. "Still not steady, but I can work with it." She rolled up her sleeves and began pouring. "My grandson is a looker too. Where is your wife tonight?"

He watched the slow, unsteady stream of coffee flow like a small waterfall into his mug.

"Now we're swimming," she said of the easy stream.

"She's passed too."

She finished pouring and placed the pot onto the floor, beside her feet. "Kids?" she asked.

"One," he replied.

The woman returned a smile. "Hope."

He sipped his coffee. "Hope," he repeated, the idea of Vän *swimming* curiously floating over his senses in a renewed way. "My wife loved swimming," he said. "She was beautiful."

The two sat quietly together for some time. After thirty minutes or so, a servant carrying a platter of champagne and chocolate-covered strawberries danced behind the counter.

"Mr. Azurite," he said. "I think someone is looking for you."

"Tell them Mr. Azurite is dealing with urgent matters," the coat check instructed.

The servant looked for confirmation. "Sir?"

Sam nodded. "Correct." He looked at the old lady, a semblance of sobriety returning. "You're good at what you do. Does anyone tell you that?"

She smiled. "Feeling better?"

"Yes," he said, and he stood up. "I'll take my coat now."

The old lady rose, folded her chair, and carried it back behind the counter. "Do you have your ticket?"

He felt around in the pockets of his tuxedo trousers. "Here it is," he said, looking down at the pink ticket for the number.

The woman smiled. "Don't tell me. Let me guess the number." She closed her eyes as if she were savoring the moment. Finally, she said, "057."

He looked at the ticket. "Nice party trick. How'd you know?" He smiled.

She pressed the rotation button on the coat rack and watched it turn. "O-Five-Seven. Here it is." Pulling his navy overcoat from its hanger, her sleeve shortened. There it was, a serial number, tattooed to her forearm.

He fixated on her tattoo, his distress growing the longer he stared. A chill ran over his body, straight into his heart. Images appeared in his head. *Dead bodies. Concentration camps. Nazis.*

She opened the door and entered the lobby with Sam's coat. Smiling, she said, "I never forget a number. *My first husband ended in O-Five-Five. My mother in O-Seven-Eight. My sister in O-Nine-Six.* Here, let me help you put it on."

She began helping him into his coat, one arm at a time.

He hesitated, then whispered in disbelief, "You survived the Holocaust?"

She was quiet; the words contorted her lips into a frown, a pain he conceptually understood, but not as deeply as he knew she did.

"Yes," she replied as she selflessly finished helping him into his coat. "I did. I did survive. And you did too in your own way, didn't you?" She smiled, redirecting the attention back to him.

"How?" He longed to know.

"How what, honey? Survive?"

He turned and took her hands into his own. Trembling as he searched her omnipotent eyes, he queried, *"How do you live without them?"*

She was quiet.

"Please," he said. "I need to know."

The old lady smiled. "Oh, that," she replied. "For a moment I thought you were trying to woo me." She winked. "You have a good heart, young man. I can tell. I can read people. I will tell you what to do, *how to live*. But you have to promise to act on it. No more drinking yourself into paralysis."

He nodded in agreement.

"How many fingers am I holding up?" she asked.

He looked at her, confused. "None," he said. "I'm holding your hands."

"Just checking," she laughed. "Now I don't want you overthinking it—it requires immediate action. It sounds simple, but first it takes some effort."

"Okay, I promise," he replied courteously.

"Bend down. I'll whisper it to you," she said. "It's not for everyone to hear, but rather, for everyone to experience."

He leaned his ear down to her coffee-and-peppermint breath of wisdom.

"How much did you love your wife?" asked the old lady.

Immediately overthinking it, he replied, "How does a person measure love?"

"Now there you go overthinking it. I thought we had a deal."

"Oh, I'm sorry," he said. "I'm trying."

She returned to his ear. "Let's reverse it. How much did your wife love you?"

His eyes grew heavy with tears.

"There's your answer," she said. "Honor her memory by honoring her heart. Open your eyes, *your heart*, to the world as though you are her vessel, sharing that love on her behalf. Dilate, as though it is your only purpose on this planet. This is the duty that we survivors of violence are left with. We absorb the light of angels." She guided him to the elevator mirror, pressed the down button, and concluded, "And with eyes as powerful and charming as yours, and with all that money that I'm sure you are making, you're a blessed child with a gift. Use your gift wisely. You have no other choice. That's all there is to it."

A chill ran over him. A memory. Red and blue lights stalled over his father's dead eyes. "My eyes are my father's eyes," he confessed. "Everyone says they are charming, but Mother used to say I got them from him."

"What color were your mother's eyes?" she questioned.

"They were blue."

She smiled. "How long have you believed that lie?"

He shrugged. "It's not a lie."

"Darling," she replied. "Your mother was protecting you. Look again."

And with that, she pecked him on the cheek, closed the elevator, and vanished back behind the racks.

PART SIX

CHAPTER THIRTY-NINE

"YOU ARE WEARING MY HAT"

I rushed to the black-and-white photograph of the baby that I had noticed the night I arrived at Handy's mysterious estate. The photograph sat on the table, just as I remembered. I threw the hat on top of my head and used it to hold back strands of wayward hair. A few pieces fell in front of my eyes anyway. I picked up the photo and examined the faces.

Think, Lanna, think.

Those eyes; I knew them somehow, from somewhere. *How old is this photograph?* I wondered. *Was this boy now a man?* I had to find him.

As I stood intensely speculating, I heard footsteps. Someone was walking up from behind. I spun around.

It was the man in the white overcoat whom I had seen in the greenhouse. "There it is," he said. "You're wearing my hat."

"Your hat?" I replied. "No, you must be mistaken. This hat belonged to my father, Jack Zar."

The man in the overcoat smiled. "Hello, Ladybug," he said.

"Ladybug?" My eyes grew wide. "How do you know my nickname?"

The man in the white overcoat smiled again and said, "I should know. I gave it to you." He laughed, placing his hands on my shoulders, and leaned in to wrap his arms around me. I pushed him away and suddenly saw sadness in his face, and I knew—"It's you."

I stepped toward him, inspecting his face. "It is you," I said again, my bottom lip quivering, my eyes filling with tears.

"I thought, if you couldn't bring yourself to come to me, then I would come to you," he said.

I put my head to his chest. His heartbeat was strong. He wrapped his arms back around me. I didn't have the emotional strength to wrap mine around him, but it didn't matter. He held me tight. I cried, ashamed. *How could I have missed it?* His shiny navy eyes, his posture; they were identical to my own.

We stood in the hallway for what felt like brief minutes but must have been for a good half hour, maybe more. I didn't want to leave. I just wanted to stand there and let him hold me forever.

He smelled like fresh aftershave, and his skin was smooth and firm, like mine. He caressed my shoulders and rubbed my back until my eyes stopped flooding. Wiping tears from my face and lifting the hair away from my eyes, he held my chin and looked into my eyes.

Suddenly I understood why no one in the house wanted to talk. I didn't want to talk anymore. I didn't care to talk. What happened didn't matter; not to me, it didn't. I was full of hope. Everything had happened so long ago. But somehow, my soul told me, it wasn't about me anymore. There were others. Finally, I pushed away, and handed him the picture.

"Explain," I said.

His body weakened and his brows furrowed. "Do you trust me?" he asked.

I did.

"First, tea." He wrapped an arm around my shoulder and nudged me toward the kitchen.

I smiled. I had waited long enough to see him. I could wait a little longer to learn the truth.

CHAPTER FORTY

A JACK IN A TEACUP

Jack filled the kettle with water, turned on the stove, and pulled a blue and white set of paisley teacups, along with a tin of jam-filled raspberry strudel, from the cabinet. He set them at the kitchen table. I sat at the table, peeled the strudel apart into smaller portions, and nibbled.

Sitting cross-legged at the table and watching me eat, he appeared a formal man. Somehow my memory hadn't pegged him that way. But there were a lot of vacancies to fill in my memory.

The kettle whistled. He rose to the stove and returned with the boiling water.

"I hope you like Chai," he said as he poured the tea into our twin paisley cups. "Sugar?"

"Yes," I said. "Please." I watched as he dropped two cubes of sugar into my cup and a dollop of honey into his.

I sipped my tea slowly, watching as he stirred his glass. I looked up at the crystal ceiling and examined the detailed moldings around it.

"So, what is it? What's going on?" I asked, attempting to cut through the silence.

He continued stirring his tea, as though watching his spoon glide through the honey could make the conversation progress as smoothly. "Ladybug, do you remember the pool—the one at the university where your mother and I would take you as a child?" he asked.

"Of course," I said. "The crowd has changed a lot since then, but it still has the same charm."

He sighed. "That's where we first met the Azurites. How old were you then?"

I shrugged. "I have no idea. Do you honestly expect me to remember?"

"I think you were around five, almost six, when I taught you to swim. Do you remember how much you loved to swim?"

A frightful memory of drowning bubbled up into my mind. "You didn't teach me," I said, and scowled. "You let me drown until I figured it out. That's not teaching. That's the literal meaning of *sink or swim*." I was immediately reminded of why I was so angry with him. Our moments together were glued to a broken past. Not one memory in our arsenal of moments shared had been current enough, or pleasant enough, to segue our relationship from past to present, and now the gaping hole between us could not be remedied with tea and strudel, no matter how comforting it was to see his face—a face that so distinctly resembled my own that it was hard not to love.

"Is that what you remember?" He laughed. But, recognizing the skepticism and sense of betrayal in my face, he turned away. "Perhaps I misremembered."

"Who the hell throws a four-year-old into a pool without a life vest?" I grumbled.

"Were you four? I thought you were at least five. I didn't do that, did I? That must have been scary for you."

"I couldn't swim. It was downright mean. Evil, even."

He raised an eyebrow. "Hmmm. Mean. That doesn't sound like me. How did you learn?"

"I sank until you came in after me."

He repeated the question. "How did you learn?"

"I used the kickboard to kick. And when it didn't work, I drowned."

"That's not how I remember it. You didn't drown. I came in after you and pulled you up. You're not dead, are you?"

"Let's agree to disagree," I said.

He continued. "I agree there is an issue of fact, but I do not agree to disagree. Is that what they teach in school? To turn the other way whenever conflict arises?"

"Says the man who chose prison over his own family," I chided in absolute contempt.

The mood grew heavy with anger.

He sighed. "Let's rewind," he said, knowing I was right. "What did I do afterwards? What did I tell you?"

"Where are you going with this?"

"I told you I would never put you in a situation from which you could not recover. Do you remember? I taught you to kick, to float, and then to kick again."

I gripped my teacup tightly. "I do not remember it that way."

"And afterwards, you taught a young boy—your first real friend—to use the board too. The two of you were opposites in many ways, but I suppose that's what attracted you to one another." He slid the picture across the table. "Do you remember the boy from your childhood?"

I released the teacup and picked up the photo. "He looks familiar. Umm …" I thought a moment. "No, I don't remember."

"You've never met the boy in this picture. This is his son."

I set the photo back down onto the table.

"Your old friend is a prominent man now. You may have heard of him."

"How prominent?" I asked.

"Prominent enough to ignore me for the rest of his life," he replied.

I raised an eyebrow. "I don't blame him. What exactly did you do to him? If you're telling the truth, how come I can't remember?"

"Do you remember coming out of your mother's womb?" he replied, making his point. "It was a long time ago." He slid the photograph back across the table. "Look closer at the boy's eyes," he said. "See if they resemble someone's."

"From a black-and-white photograph?" I asked skeptically.

"I keep thinking, *I know those eyes. They're blue. So blue. The bluest.* But I can't place him."

He chuckled. "Your soul wants to remember, but your brain is in your way. This boy here has brown eyes, yet they mimic the intensity of his father's. They're, as you'd phrase it, *brown, so brown, the brownest.*"

I took a deep breath.

"Are you ready to learn the truth?" he asked, mirroring my deep breath with one of his own.

"Yes," I determined. But I had a feeling I was going to need a lot more of those breaths.

CHAPTER FORTY-ONE

CONFESSION

My father told me about Sophie; about how we had met at the pool, about how she and my mother had grown close, and how Mother sometimes invited her to the cottage for tea. Then he told me about Sophie's husband, Nico.

"Sophie was always fearful," he said. "She believed Nico loved her, even when he abused her."

"Did he?"

"What do *you* think?" he replied.

"No," I said. "But she loved him anyway, didn't she?"

"Yes," he said. "She wanted so badly to believe in his goodness, so much so that she turned away from his darker side. And, sometimes, there was goodness. That's why it was so tricky. He was tricky."

"I grew fond of her," he continued. "She and her son would visit us at the pool whenever Nico was away on business. She was mysterious. She had this indestructible persistence to her personality. She loathed the way Nico treated her, but she felt that the only way to stay alive was to placate him. And this, though horrifying, sometimes satisfied her in some peculiar way. She was a woman who took pride in small victories. Sam's purse filled with notebooks, his love of math—these little things allowed Sam to survive. You could say that she was perhaps the reason why he is one of the most powerful men on earth today. You were fond of her, too. She had a way about her. Do you remember either of them?" he asked.

"I don't remember," I said. "But," I paused. "There is something unusual I've been thinking of lately ..." I told him of my vision about a tall, lonely man with black-tar eyes and a son.

"That's Sam, all right," he said, and told me the rest of his story. "One night, I bumped into Sophie. She was standing outside in line at a homeless shelter. She was hiding from Nico. I insisted she spend the night at our house, or at least at a hotel."

My stomach churned.

"She refused. Said he'd canceled her credit card. Finally, I told her that if she wasn't going to stay with us, I was going to take her to a hotel and pay for her stay, but first we were going to fill out a new application for a credit card. I cosigned. I wanted to help her get away. I spent the night with her. I couldn't leave her like that."

"Did you have sex with her?"

"Yes. We had an affair," he said sternly, as though he had been practicing the line.

I gasped. "Why?"

"It was a one-time thing. But, to answer your question: out of pity, out of humanity. I was not thinking clearly. And because I loved her."

"You loved her?" I retorted. "What about Mother? What about me? Was that humane?"

"Ladybug, you have to understand," he said, trying to quell my anger. "I was very insecure. Your mother and I had been so busy with you two girls that we had already grown distant. Seeing Sophie's desperation made it worse."

"That's an excuse," I said angrily, knowing that the only correct response was an apology.

"I'm sorry," he said immediately. "I didn't mean to rattle you. I know that an affair is something difficult to digest. Seeing Sophie endure such mercilessness awakened a sort of sadness within me. I questioned myself, my own worthiness. How could I get her out? I self-destructed. Seeing her that way, I knew she needed love, and I wanted to give it to her. I made a mistake. Then I purchased the gun. Can you imagine? Me—I purchased a gun. It was supposed to be a last resort, only for her to use in self-defense in the worst of circumstances and only to distract. I never believed he would—" He could not bring himself to finish the sentence.

Sadness rushed over me as I thought of Mother, and of Sophie. *Was it Nico who had done this to my family? Or was it my father?*

"What about Mom?" I asked. "Does she know the real story?"

His spirit darkened. "It disturbed the very essence of her being in the moment and for a long time after. Years. Decades. She has now come to terms with it, though I have yet to come to peace with it fully myself. That's why I am here; I suppose that's obvious."

I felt sick to my stomach. "Did you ever love Mom?"

"I did, and I still do. She's hard not to love. But I did the unthinkable. I took away what was most precious between us. Trust. I dragged her into something beyond repent or repair. I lost two loves. One murdered, shot dead, her red hair pulled right from her head over the credit card application that I had filled out for her. The other, your mother, I transformed into a vessel of self-loathing and self-sacrifice. Plea bargain or not, I wanted to go to prison for what happened to Sophie, for what I did to your mother. And now I see, to you. He covered his eyes, embarrassed by the tears streaming down his face. "But I was too stupid. Even with all my academic conquests and papers, you girls loved me, and yet, how little I loved myself. I could have found another way."

I began sobbing. "Mother would have forgiven you," I said, the tears pouring from my eyes as though they had been imprisoned for twenty years and the guard had finally opened the gates, only to realize they were not convicts, they were regular people.

"You are correct," he said. "But in exchange for what?"

"I don't know," I said. I reached for his hand, held it, and squeezed tightly.

"Her dignity," he cried. "Her dignity. And that is just not a fair trade."

"No, you're right. It's not," I whimpered with him. "It's okay," I told him. "I love you." I wasn't sure it was true, but I knew I wanted the hurt to stop. And then I realized, *I do love him.*

A serene smile emerged on his face, as though my forgiveness had lifted the weight off him. He paused, took some deep breaths, and cautiously asked, "Can you do something for me?"

I tensed.

"That little boy, Sam, is now a man. He was your first real friend. You are connected. You cannot deny yourself of this. He lives in your dreams. Will you—"

Shep appeared in the kitchen doorway. As usual, he looked as though he had just walked out of a photo shoot in his blue jeans and pressed white T-shirt that matched the pure whites of his eyes. I wiped my face, embarrassed by my tears, but, relieved to see him again, I rose to hug him.

He slid his fingers through mine and looked curiously into my eyes.

"I missed you," I said. "For some reason, I thought you weren't ever coming back."

His eyes shimmered. He squeezed my hand. "I missed you too," he replied, and I could see he was holding back the urge to kiss me by the funny way he was smiling and gawking at my lips. "You're stuck with me."

My father interrupted. "Ahem."

Shep smiled, in that aroused and intrepid way that I assumed all men did when looking at another man's adult daughter. Stepping away, he muttered a low and respectful "Hello, Jack."

I jabbed Shep flirtatiously in the shoulder, nudged him back to the door, and hoped he would get the message that Father and I needed the space and time to reconcile years of absence and heartache. Together, we awkwardly waited while Shep proceeded to pull a picnic basket and a blanket out from the center isle of the kitchen's island cupboards. Shep began methodically filling the basket with crackers, cheese, peaches, cherries, tomatoes (which he stopped to dice into a sort of bruschetta) and a bottle of bubbly water, all while Father and I hovered silently and impatiently nearby. When Shep finally completed the basket, he courteously waved us over to join him, but the both of us, without appetite, declined the invitation. This is when a jarring thought occurred to me: *How much about my life—my existence—did Shep already know?*

Suddenly, I felt exposed. It was as though I were in a bad teen sitcom, and Kelly and Jessie, two female characters from the '90s television hit show *Saved by the Bell*, had gathered with the other perky, popular kids—blond-haired, blue-eyed Zack Morris and muscleman Slater—along with my real-life guidance counselor, my shrink, and Mr. Belding (the school's principal) to discuss how grossly unqualified I was to be with a man as kind and as handsome as him.

I tended to my cup of tea and beckoned my father to rejoin me at the table. Shep walked over and pecked me sweetly on the head. "Goodbye," he said, picnic basket and blanket in hand.

I rolled my shoulder coldly away from him, perturbed by the idea that he had been keeping something monumental from me—that he knew all of my failures, or worse, that he saw my failures the way *they*, the cyclone of speculators from my past life, had.

Shep appeared perplexed and maybe even hurt by my cold shoulder as he left the room, but I still couldn't shake the sinking feeling.

"Don't be like me," my father said, once Shep was gone. "Don't destroy love."

"I'm not like you," I responded. "Nothing about me is like you."

He looked down, and I could tell instantly that I had hurt his feelings, possibly in a way that I would never understand. "I'm sorry," I said genuinely. "I don't know why I said that."

"Do you resent me?" he asked, looking pleadingly into my eyes.

I wasn't sure; the space between us seemed wide again. Finally, I pushed past it and said, "I resent loving you, but I think it will pass."

"Ladybug," he said with an air of confidence. "There is something very important I want you to do. I want you to go to Sam Azurite. He needs you. He won't speak to me. He's led a difficult life all these years."

I rolled my eyes.

"There's more to the story than you know," he replied, and went on. "His wife came looking for me, years ago."

"Let me guess; you slept with her, too," I maligned.

He replied dismissively, "No. She came looking for me but didn't find me. Instead, she found a—" He paused, thinking about how to refer to him. "A colleague."

"Call him what he is. A cellmate."

"Yes, a friend."

"Go on."

"He told her I was gone. That some rich man had sprung me."

"And did he?"

"Who?"

"Handy," I said. "Did Handy spring you?"

"Yes, but it's not what you think."

I could sense more disappointment coming.

"I'm sorry to disappoint you," he said. "I'm not special. I merely befriended someone in the program who is special, and she found a way to sponsor me. But, then again, none of us are." He grinned. "By the way, what do you know about Shep?"

"I know enough," I lied, feeling belittled. "What does all this have to do with me?"

His demeanor intensified. "Sam's wife died here." He looked blankly into my eyes.

"*Here?*" I repeated, confused, conflicted.

He continued. "God or fate or free will, or whatever you believe in, brought her here. She birthed her baby boy in the daffodil field where you spend your evenings. She died during childbirth. There was a storm. Her pickup truck hit a boulder and she died shortly after delivering her son. And this is where you come in. Sam needs help. He may be looking for you; only, he doesn't know it."

Shivers ran up my spine. "Did I know her?"

"Regretfully, neither of us did."

"Why me?" I asked. "Why not you?"

"Because you have history."

"So?" I questioned. "You have history too."

"And I sent letters."

"So what?"

"He didn't respond."

"I've read your letters; I know why he didn't respond— you're always talking about the past as though we are children. You should know something, Dad. Wait." I paused. "I don't understand. How did she find this place? What are the odds?"

His navy eyes sparked like someone had lit a match. "Precisely the question I hoped you'd ask," he said. "I don't think she knew where she was going. I think her subconscious brought her here."

He scanned my face to see if I was connecting the dots. "Magical things happen during childbirth, Ladybug. Consciousness is like an ocean. We are all part of it. Our thoughts are part of it. Sometimes it carries us where we need to go, even if it is not where we want to go."

"I still don't understand," I said.

"She read my letters. And she used to write to me, to the same P.O. box that I visited every week to see if you had written to me. She knew something was bothering Sam— something he couldn't put words to—and though he believed he was permanently damaged, she believed what ailed him was temporary. And perhaps that is the biggest irony, that her time here on earth was so brief. She believed that if she could bring us together—you and me with Sam, it would relieve him and bring the two of them closer together. For the sake of their unborn (but now born) child. That's what she said in her letters. That's all I knew about her. How she found this place, that was fate."

"Wow. What do you want me to do, exactly? Why me?"

"I created pain," he said. "You will create hope."

"It doesn't feel right," I told him.

"It will," he replied.

"No," I stated firmly. "I don't want to. No more schemes. I'm an adult woman. I can't live in your past forever." And with that, I stood up, shoved my chair under the table, and furiously left the room.

CHAPTER FORTY-TWO

WHOSE PAWN AM I THIS TIME?

Am I supposed to feel better? I contemplated, fuming. I'm not a pawn. I'm a person. Does anyone give a shit about what I want?

Seeing Jack was supposed to make things better, but in some ways, I felt worse. I ducked into my bedroom and sat on the bed, filled with rage.

Enough of this. I have to get out of here. I slipped out of the delicate linen dress that Setara had given me, made my bed, and laid the dress across it. I opened the closet, where my black pants and shirt hung perfectly laundered. My stilettos sat on the floor beneath them. I was not looking forward to wearing them again. From now on, I told myself, I'm going to start wearing boots. I feel grounded in boots. No more stilettos.

I dressed myself in black, threw my shoes into my tote, and rushed out of the house to confront Shep in the daffodil field.

Sitting underneath a tree, reading a book, Shep looked up and smiled. Seeing me in my work garb, a look of concern washed over his face. He stood to greet me.

"I've had it," I told him, ignoring house rules. "Thank you for all you've done for me, but I'm calling it quits. I don't want to be here any longer. I miss my life. I don't know how much you know, but you made a fool of me by hiding the facts. I want you to take me home."

He tried to calm me. "Hey," he said, grabbing the tote from my shoulder and attempting to set it down. "Sit a minute. Tell me what's wrong."

"It's all a trick," I said. "No more games."

"What's a trick?" he asked. "Who's tricking you?"

I was so livid, I couldn't speak. I needed the anger to go somewhere. I fisted a large bushel of daffodil-heads and ripped them out of the ground, out of their bodies, as though they were mine and I was entitled to do whatever reckless harm I wanted to them. Nature had done us wrong; it needed to pay. Teeming and beating and feeding and teething, nature was violent, and I was tired of being its victim. Why had Sophie ever existed? Why had Nico? Why had Father loved her? Why had Mother trusted him? Why had it taken Nguyen? Why had it brought us here? Why was I left with its heavy debt? I ran to the boulders near the edge of the field, lifted one off the ground, and threw it, as though throwing it could crack me in half and I could take back my life.

But the anger would not come out. It was stuck like a rusted bolt to a steel beam and I needed a hammer to chip away slowly at it. I screamed and screamed. I screamed until Shep pulled me to the ground and held me tightly as though he were the hammer.

"Let go of me," I said, pushing him off. But I did not mean it. I wanted him there; I needed him there.

"Let go," I repeated, waking to the severity of my behavior.

He waited a few seconds until I was still, and then let go.

I pulled his arms back and took a deep breath. "No, hold me. Just hold me," I said. "I'm sorry. I didn't mean it." The sun warmed my cheeks. The smell of damaged flowers filled my nostrils. He held me tightly.

"Tell me what happened."

I gulped another breath. "Words hurt," I said. "I want to go home. I'm ready to leave now."

"Okay," he said.

I could see in his eyes that he was hurt by my sadness, but I stood up, grabbed my shoes and tote, and set off toward the house like an escaped zoo animal. He quickly packed his picnic basket and trailed behind. When he finally caught up, I was already sitting in the pickup, vividly imagining a deceased woman laboring, probably in this truck I was now sitting in. It gave me goose bumps. Everything around me was part of an inherited past. I needed to return to the present.

Shep walked to the truck and opened the door to where I was sitting. "We'll go another way," he said. He shook a set of keys in front of my face, and with an I-have-access-to-expensive-things sort of smile, said, "I have the keys to the helicopter."

"Of course you do." I rolled my eyes.

A shiver ran down my spine. "Where'd you get this truck?" I asked, longing for confirmation.

"This old thing?" he responded. "Don't know. It's been around here for a while. It's sort of a family truck, I guess."

"Family" was all I needed to hear to know what that meant, but I couldn't tell if he was lying, if he knew. Something told me he didn't. And that gave me a moment of relief—and a glimmer of excitement.

CHAPTER FORTY-THREE

HOW MUCH DO YOU KNOW?

When the chopper landed in the yard outside our family cottage, which is, by the way, something I never thought I would say, Mother did not seem at all alarmed. The noise from the propeller drew her into the yard, where she met us with an omniscient smile.

Shep slid off his sexy silver aviators, dropped the stairs, and pounced out. He held out his hand. "Watch your step," he said, reaching for my hand. I slipped my palm in his hand and held on to it long after I had exited.

When I saw my mother, I let go. Her face seemed lighter, happier. Suddenly I was overcome by how much I had missed her. "Hi, Mom," I said, as I embraced her. She held me closely, as though she had missed me too, and then quickly let go.

"This is Shep," I said, walking him over to her. He bowed and held out his hand.

"I hear you are quite the gentleman," she said in her tender maternal voice.

He blushed.

"How much do you know?" I asked.

"Mothers know everything," she said. "What will you do?"

"What do you mean?" I replied.

"Will you help?" she asked.

"Help who?" I responded.

She smiled easily. "You know who. Yourself."

Perplexed, I stood in silence.

"What do *you* want?" she asked.

What do I want? I wondered.

I searched Shep's eyes, as though his corneas could rationalize for me, but instead I found only kindness and curiosity, and this carried me into a new reality.

"I want peace. Peace of mind. Peace of heart," I finally said.

"What will give you that?" Mother asked.

I don't know, I thought.

"By the way," she said. "Your boss has been calling nonstop. I covered for you."

I shrugged.

"I told her we had a family emergency."

"What did she say?"

"She said to do what you need to do and that when you are ready, your job would still be waiting."

"Nice," I replied. "That seems unlike her. Did she—"

"Then she made a racist remark," she continued. "Something about, if you didn't return to the office, she would have you checked by Immigration."

I cringed and laughed. "Yep, that's her, all right."

She raised an eyebrow.

"I've been trying to quit," I explained. "But she keeps sucking me back in. Listen, not to deflect, but do you know where Sam Azurite lives?" I asked, curiously scanning her face for her reaction. "I know it's a weird, out-of-the-blue question, but I think I might need to see him."

"Why's that?" she said. "He's not too far from here. I've been saving his address for you, for this moment."

"Do you always know what I will do before I do it?"

She smiled. "Of course. I'm your mother."

I turned to Shep. "I think I'm good now. Will you come back for me?"

"Are you sure," he replied, "you don't want me to come along?"

"I'm sure," I said, and then pushed away. Suddenly I felt strangely powerful. I bit my lips cutely. "I'm positive," I repeated. "I'm a woman of New York City, a vessel of hope, and, by the way, I love you."

I turned and began walking away as though I didn't need to hear him say it back, and the best part was: I *didn't* need to hear him say it back. I was proud of who I was and proud to love him.

Shep grabbed me by the waist and pulled me into his hard, hot body. "Not so fast, *you*," he said, and he tasted my lips with his own. We both lingered in pheromones, taking in one another's lips and tongues, both belonging to ourselves and to one another. My body yearned to be one with him. Yet, we already were.

The summer wind had dulled the essence of our kiss only briefly as my curly bangs blew into our mouths, and Mother, who had walked up ahead, stood uncomfortably waiting. Had she not, we would have done a lot more than kiss.

But, "Ahem, I'm still here," Mother reminded, and we dismounted from one another, blushing.

I lost myself in his eyes for one moment longer, reveling in the freedom of being vulnerable and without fear. "I want to see you every day for the rest of my life," I told him. "Does that make you uncomfortable? I hope so."

He smiled, his eyes glimmering. "Your loving me feels right. I love you, and I want that too."

I smiled and pecked him on the lips again, wanting to take him in, but I stopped and exhaled. "There's something I need to take care of on my own."

He nodded.

Then I turned away, unwound my hair tie, and let the wind bring me to Mother.

He skipped back up the stairs to the helicopter and called out, "When will I see you again?" with the whimsical excitement that only true love can bring.

"In a week. In the City. You know where I work. Don't bring any guests!" I joked.

He waited until we were a safe distance away, reeled the stairs back up, hopped into the pilot's seat, geared up, and started the propeller.

Mother and I watched the helicopter as it disappeared into the horizon.

"I love that man," I said aloud to myself.

Mother winked. "There's my girl."

CHAPTER FORTY-FOUR

CONVERSATIONS WITH THE MOON

As dusk turned to dawn, I sat under my favorite tree, imbibing the tropical heat of summer, my body still tingling from the taste of Shep's apple-flesh. In the comfort of my own thoughts, I marinated on what must have been a lonely life for the young orphan Sam Azurite, my estranged brother in spirit—would he ever know it? It seems, perhaps, that person in my vision with hollow eyes had actually been me too. I had abandoned my father and violated my own soul by accepting the penetration of unworthy lovers, and yet my train wreck of a life was panning out okay. Was his?

I wondered, *would he remember me? Would I be able to help him? Did he even need my help?*

Sophie. She was so beautiful. Her red rose hair. And her gleaming skin.

What was Nguyen like? Was Sophie anything like her?

That night, the Moon shone brightly. As I gazed into the starlit sky, I wondered *why had I rejected my father for so long? Didn't I know I was lucky to have one?*

I sighed, disappointed with myself. I had done to my father exactly what everyone had done to me. I had boxed him in and labeled him. I had psyched him out of my mind, erased everything we had between us, and discarded him like a piece of garbage. It was no surprise that, slithering through life, I had attracted maggots. I had assaulted myself into believing that I no longer loved my father, extracting the possibility of seeing love from my very own existence. It was time I released myself of this burden. And my mother—*how long had I been saving a woman who didn't need saving?*

Now I had friends. I had love. If I was gifted with an opportunity to be *hope* to somebody—to my father, to Sam, or his son—then maybe I could be hope to me too. If showing up at his doorstep would set Jack free, then maybe it would set me free too. I was in. All in.

The sky blackened and thunder struck, followed quickly by lightning and heavy rain. The trail back to Mother's cottage flooded. I smiled. Maybe I would finally get to see the flagellates in the basement. I wondered—*would Shep love the cavern as much as I had?* Of course he would. How could he not? I couldn't wait to at last share it.

I rushed back to the cottage, but for one more moment I stopped along the path to take cover under the leafy umbrella-like branches of one of the more magnificent pine trees along the trail back. Standing in place just long enough to outline a new route through the woods toward the cottage, the Moon pulsed, luring me to take notice of it again before I ran inside.

"Remember the feeling of floating in water. Remember the sun," it glowed.

Suddenly, it came to me. "The water wants to help you," my father had told me as a wide-eyed child. "You need to create space within."

I smirked. It was *that* simple. "The water wants to help."

"Here I am, world!" I sang out, and 1-2-3, I bounced from puddle to puddle, the rain pounding hard against my body as I tangoed with it.

"Let there be space!" I sang out. The wind pushed me fast, and before I could bounce once more, I was in through the screen door, kicking off my flip-flops, skidding across the floor like Elvis Presley and stripping naked to my bare skin. My hair drizzled rainwater from my clavicles down and over my hardened nipples, and I hopped into my springy bed and wrapped myself in cotton sheets, no longer tangled by my childhood. I drifted to sleep remembering an easier time. A time when the air smelled like a raspberry picked straight from the branch and the mountains reached high above the cotton-candy clouds.

I was finally home.

CHAPTER FORTY-FIVE

ONWARD

The very next morning—early, at 5 a.m.—I showered, brushed my teeth, and headed down to the kitchen with a sense of willfulness and purpose I had long forgotten. I slept well and woke with anticipation. Mother was still asleep.

I opened the fridge and pulled out eggs and kale. I filled the coffeemaker with fresh vanilla-bean coffee and set it for two.

The eggs sizzled as I flipped them over easy. I felt badly about eating them, and wasn't quite sure why, but I did. I added cumin, turmeric, red pepper, salt, and crushed saffron. In a separate pot, I cooked the kale in sunflower oil with salt and white peppercorn until it was nice and soft. I added sunflower seeds for texture, and laid the perfectly cooked eggs on top in two separate dishes, one for me, one for Mother. I covered hers with a lid.

I sat at the kitchen table alone, drinking coffee, eating breakfast, and daydreaming about Shep's deep-sunken eyes and his firm masculine body. When I finished, I grabbed a white porcelain tray with a multicolored peacock design, and placed the dish for Mother together with a fresh cup of coffee. For a special touch, I plucked a dandelion from the garden, which, though frequently thought of as a weed, Mother had allowed in some areas of the grass because it had medicinal properties when drank as tea, and I carried it back, plopped it into a small vase, and added it to the tray.

I shoveled through odds and ends in the kitchen junk drawer to find a pen and paper, and found both.

"Thank you for everything," I wrote on the paper. "I'm sorry about what Dad did to you. I love you and I promise to start visiting more. How you raised me with what little you had—you make me proud. I was so angry *for you* that I forgot to heal. Can you believe that? Mary must think I'm a real idiot. Don't tell her I said that. I'll be back with the car sometime this afternoon, if not sooner. Lanna."

I placed the note on the tray, walked it to her room, and set the tray onto the nightstand next to Mother's bed.

The floorboard creaked as I was sliding away. I stopped in the doorway to look back.

She opened one eye and smiled. "Is that breakfast I smell?"

I came in and sat down. "I'm heading out for a bit," I whispered. "Do you mind if I take the car?"

She winked. "Go ahead."

"Breakfast is on the nightstand," I said. I kissed her on the cheek, grabbed the car keys, set the GPS, and took off.

Forty-five minutes later, I arrived at Sam's gorgeous, intimidating house. From the outside, it was clear he had done well. My heart beat wildly. *What am I doing here?* I couldn't bring myself to pull into the driveway. It all seemed so ridiculous and overwhelming at the same time.

I decided to wait. It was still early, 7 a.m.

Twenty more minutes passed, and I parked the car on the side of the street, deciding not to pull in yet. I stepped out for a morning stretch. Yawning, I reached my arms overhead into the first of many Vinyasa poses.

A woman in her fifties, wearing round spectacles and a sleeveless plaid V-neck sweater, pulled her Mercedes out from a neighbor's driveway and caught me standing in the street doing yoga poses.

"Are you lost?" she asked in that "what-is-this-freak-doing-on-my-street?" sort of way.

I dismounted from my pose and placed both hands over my hips. "Not anymore," I smiled. "I'm visiting a friend. It's a surprise, but I think it might be too soon. I mean, *early*."

She shot me a dubious look. "If I find out you're a reporter—I've taken down your license plate number."

"No, I'm not. I'm a friend. Promise," I responded.

She softened. "Oh, okay; well, they're usually up and out early. You can ring the bell. They're probably awake."

"Thanks," I said.

"How do you know them?" she said suspiciously, before pulling away.

"Long story," I replied. "Some might say we grew up together."

"I've got my eye on you," she said, as she pulled off and down the cleanly paved road.

Sheesh, I thought. *Friendly*. I hopped back into the driver's seat. I still wasn't sure I was ready to knock on the door. I yawned and looked at my watch.

7:05 a.m. Ugh. I popped open the glove compartment in search of goodies—books, brochures, magazines, lollipops, almonds—anything. There was nothing interesting. Then I came across a cookie.

CHAPTER FORTY-SIX

THE BUS IS COMING

A cheery little boy about the age of seven or eight, with regal brown eyes and straight black hair, wearing a collared shirt, green tweed blazer, and a pair of beige khakis, knocked on my window. "Hey, lady, you can't park here. This is where the bus stops," he said with a squeaky, high-pitched voice.

I pulled down the window. "Sorry, kid."

"Why're you sitting here, anyway?" asked the boy.

"No reason," I said. "Just exploring, got tired, decided to stop. Do you like to explore?"

The boy scratched his head. "Not really."

"Oh," I said, surprised. "What *do* you like to do?"

The boy thought for a moment and smiled. "Swim!" he said enthusiastically.

"You do?" I said. "I like to swim too! How often do you go?"

His glow dimmed. "Not often," he said.

"Too bad," I replied. "Maybe I can take you. Is your dad home?"

"I think so," he said. "He was supposed to drive me today, but he didn't get out of bed. I think he's sick. "

"You're not sure?" I asked.

"He smells bad. Like alcohol. He came home late."

"Oh," I said.

"He doesn't usually do that," the boy said. "He says it's not good for work."

"Makes sense," I said.

"Do you know my dad?" he asked.

"Sort of," I said. "We were friends when we were both little."

He laughed. "Yeah, right. Dad was never little."

I smiled. "Why's that?"

"Haven't you seen him? He's huge, and he works all the time. Did he work all the time then, too?"

Suddenly regaling in a memory of Sam carrying a purse and winding his silly protractor along with his graph books, I smiled. "Actually, yes. He worked most of the time, but not all. Believe it or not, we used to have a lot of fun together."

"You must not have been around long," he said perceptively. "You should probably move your car. I can see the bus coming."

"Right," I said, and started the engine. "Hey, do you want me to drive you to school?"

He scratched his head.

I continued. "If your dad says it's okay?"

He nodded. "Sure."

"Okay, what's your name?"

"It's Vän."

"Like a vehicle?"

He shook his head yes. "Don't make fun of me."

"Make fun of you? Why would I do that? Do people do that to you? They're stupid. It's an awesome name. I'll meet you in the driveway." I pulled into the driveway and parked. He followed behind. I reopened the glove compartment and grabbed a pen and pad. "Can you bring him this?"

"Sure," he said.

"I'm outside," I wrote on the pad. "I'm Lanna. Do you remember me? We used to swim together as kids."

I folded the note in half and handed it to Vän. He opened it, looked back up at me, smiled, and took it inside. While waiting, I checked myself out in the mirror, wondering if Sam would even be able to recognize me. I hadn't been able to recognize my own father.

A few minutes later, a very tall man in a white robe, with intense blue eyes and wavy brown hair, appeared at the front door. He ran his fingers through his hair and stepped halfway through the door.

"What do you want from me?" he asked firmly.

I could smell the alcohol oozing from his pores, even as I sat in the car. I fumbled for the door handle, got out, and approached the stairs. Suddenly, I was struck by how his voice had transformed from that of an awkward young boy to an attractive executive male model. Even hung-over in a robe, he looked as though he had walked out of a Saks catalog. What could I possibly say or do that would make this man want me near? And what was the purpose of my visit? To cheer him up? I felt stupid.

"I'm not sure," I said steadily, taking in his appearance as I approached. "All of this is new to me. I guess I just wanted to see if you were okay." I gleaned his facial reaction. He looked as though he was nursing a bad headache. "Are you?"

"Who told you to come here?" he asked, pressing his fingers against his temples. "Was it Bill? Why are you really here?"

I paused for a minute, not knowing how to answer. Soaking in the sunshine and searching for the right words, I finally came up with an answer. "To float," I said softly. "To float. That's all. I'm here because I want to float. I'm tired of drowning. I heard through the grapevine that you might be tired too."

"To float?" he repeated. He stood in silence. After a moment, a smile emerged. He slowly opened the door and stepped onto the stoop.

"What did you say?" he asked again, inspecting my eyes as though the concept had riddled him in a positive way.

I gazed into his eyes, surrendering to the old but new familiar face and remembering our kindred friendship. "To *float*. I want to *float* with you. That's all I want." I was trembling.

The boy reached for his father's hand. "Can she bring me to school today?"

He held my gaze. "Let me get cleaned up first," he replied. "Want to play hooky today?" he said, turning toward his son.

"Yes!" the boy exclaimed.

"Come on, then. Let's do this. Let's float."

I grinned. "Like a friend?"

"Something like that," Sam replied.

* * *

I know what you're thinking—why did my spontaneous re-emergence in Sam's life matter? And I'd like to tell you there's one answer. But there are too many answers. What I can tell you is that when someone cares enough about you to show up, and he or she escorts you from where you are to wherever you need to be, they're probably worth keeping around. And if you're truly lucky, you may find that a chance encounter with a compassionate coat attendant is as good, if not better, than a drive through the woods to a meditation camp run by a billionaire. But if all else fails and you are alone, never stop believing in skies that change color and the feeling of floating in water.

DEDICATIONS & GRATITUDES

This book is dedicated to the universe and to all its magnificent seekers of wisdom and truth. May you prosper; may you find your spouses, your soul mates, and your friends; may your passions be your happiness; may you feel safe to crumble; may you be free.

This book is also dedicated to lost wonderers and curiosity junkies who are trying to understand how life works. In the words of the prolific Mark Twain: "It ain't what you don't know that gets you into trouble. It's what you know for sure that just ain't so."

To my husband and best friend, Evan Fensterstock: Thank you for your glowing existence and for encouraging me to write this book. You're a wonderful husband, a loving father to our child, and a true gentleman—attractive, funny, athletic, giving, compassionate, and so much more. Thank you for embarking on this parenting journey with me and for coaching me through labor. Thank you for listening to my list of ongoing demands, and doing every darn thing you can to meet them, despite how insurmountable it sometimes seems. You are an amazing soul. Can you believe we met on Halloween? The way you furrowed your brows like an adorable mountain lion; that white suit that could make Don

Johnson jealous, and the silly, suspicious way we gazed at one another, as though we were both asking, "Am I dreaming?" Whoosh. Unforgettable. Do you remember how on our first date, I said, "I missed you," and I looked into your eyes as if I had known you my entire life. It was destiny. Thank you for choosing to spend your grand life with little nobody-somebody me.

To my younger sister, Nika: Thank you for always putting me up on a pedestal, even when I am ashamed of my own existence. You have blossomed into the most remarkable young woman—funny, perceptive, clever, generous, gorgeous, and the list goes on. Remember that time we lived together in Cambridge in that slanted apartment invaded by mice? Well, I hereby promise never again to trick you into believing those mice are in your head. Nika, you are a special soul with a gifted heart, and I am so grateful to have you in my life. I can honestly say that without you, there'd be no me.

To my intellectual, spiritual, and biological mother, Roya: Where do I begin? Oh, okay, I've got it. Mom, thank you for pushing me through your vagina. I know from experience how incredibly painful that is. Thank you for putting clothes on my back and food in my belly. Thank you for being smarter than me in all the right ways, and for teaching me to observe, to read, to write, to meditate, and to reflect. How you managed to do what you've done from sea to sea when English was not your first language is astonishing to me. How you manage to be in more than one place at one time and all the time is magic, frightening, and profoundly beautiful. Thank you for your unending fountain of love. For moving mountains to give me this life. I promise you, I won't let you down: I will always live it to the very fullest, and I love you more than you will ever know.

To my stepfather, Joel, whose many talents have allowed me to witness the limitlessness of human creativity: Joel, thank you for spending countless hours singing and writing music with me, for sharing your delight for literature and art, and for always humoring my intellect with more questions than answers.

To my editor, Cindy Hochman of "100 Proof" Copyediting Services: You are, by leaps and bounds, the best editor I have ever known. Through punctuation, you taught me how to build a story within a story within a story. I cannot believe how lucky I am to have pursued your services on a whim. Talk about the stars aligning. Thank you for being so passionate about editing.

And, finally, to my soft-spoken and patient father, Masoud, who loved me until the day he died, and filled my life with questions. Masoud, I see you in the sky and feel you in the wind. I forgive you. I am so sorry it took me so long to come around. *Can you hear me?*

AFTERWORD

Someone once posited that the laws of attraction are binding. What does that mean? I suppose I know what it means. I suppose it means that we are all simple human beings drawn to one another by a great and masterful puppeteer. God. Love. Consciousness. Call it what you will.

This seems fairly logical, does it not? After all, we enter the universe in one massive particle of beautiful and incompetent messiness. Something forces us out of the womb like Chief Justice herself.

And now that we are here, people make mistakes. People marry. People cheat. People kill. People run. People die. People redeem themselves. Our givers vanish, but our cries don't, and we continue sending signals of hope and despair, like we always have; only, whom, if anyone, are we bound to attract? And who, if anyone, inherits the debts of our givers?

I suppose *we* do, don't we? We inherit those debts, as all generations before us have, but sometimes—no, most of the time—our wires cross, and like all contracts, they are open to interpretation.

ABOUT THE AUTHOR

Tara Makhmali is an Iranian-born U.S. citizen whose family left Iran shortly after the revolution. She lives in Hoboken, New Jersey, with her husband, Evan, a prominent New York City litigator, their beautiful daughter, Sydney, and their miniature English bulldog, Wilson. Tara holds a Bachelor of Arts degree in English from the University of Massachusetts in Boston. She is a certified PMP who has worked in various capacities from Project Manager to Recruiter to Consultant for notable companies such as Pearson Publishing, FCB Advertising, Bridgewater Associates, and HBO. In her spare time, she plays guitar and classical piano. Above all, she is a curious person who cares deeply for people and progress.